THE
GUNMASTER

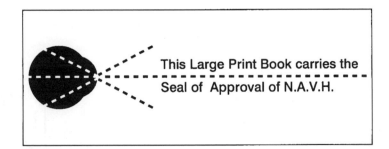

This Large Print Book carries the
Seal of Approval of N.A.V.H.

THE GUNMASTER

Ray Hogan

G.K. Hall & Co. • Thorndike, Maine

Published in 2001 by arrangement with Golden West Literary Agency.

G.K. Hall Large Print Western Series.

The text of this Large Print edition is unabridged.
Other aspects of the book may vary from the original edition.

Set in 16 pt. Plantin.

Printed in the United States on permanent paper.

Library of Congress Cataloging-in-Publication Data

Hogan, Ray, 1908–
   The gunmaster / Ray Hogan.
      p.   cm.
   ISBN 0-7838-9353-1 (lg. print : hc : alk. paper)
   1. Outlaws — Fiction. 2. Kidnapping — Fiction. 3. United States
marshals — Fiction. 4. Large type books. I. Title.
PS3558.O3473 G79 2001
   813'.54—dc21   00-053845

THE
GUNMASTER

1

He came out of the Dakotas, riding south, a tall, quiet man with shrewd eyes and hawklike features. He was on a long-legged sorrel, and the double-rigged saddle he forked showed wear, as did the pistol on his hip.

He saw the three men moving up on his trail when he crossed the Colorado-Arkansas but gave little thought to it; the frontier, in that feverish year of 1880, was a vast sea with the populace shifting restlessly back and forth like a continuous tide, and it was entirely normal to encounter itinerants on the once seldom-traveled roads.

But a day later, when he entered New Mexico Territory not far from the mountain known as Capulin, Aaron Ledbetter got the feeling the trio were more than ordinary pilgrims; they were closing in on him in a relentless, determined manner — and much too fast. Drifters, or men pulling stakes in search of the promised land, didn't push their horses so hard.

Halting in the brush on the south side of the *sierra grande,* he let his flat gaze settle on the distant figures. If they sought him it likely had something to do with the shooting scrape he had been forced into at Monument City. There had been a loud, smart-mouthed man named Rosen who fancied himself quite a hand with a pistol, and tried to prove it.

It had been a fair contest, resolved simply on the basis of speed and unerring accuracy, and Ledbetter, were he the sort who recorded gruesome statistics, could have carved another notch in the cedar handles of his forty-five Colt's.

But to him it was no feat to be in any way memorialized; it was instead only another link in a seemingly endless chain of effort aimed at self-preservation. He'd had no quarrel with Rosen, just as there had been none with the others who had fallen victim to his incredible skill, but the calm self-assurance, the aura of invincibility that clung to him, seemed to bestir belligerence in some and egg the more intrepid into braving his weapon.

A curious mixture of good and bad, Aaron Ledbetter was the son of a wealthy upstate New York family. He had found no liking for paternal enterprises, however successful, and at fifteen had taken his leave of the mansion and shortly after found himself a tidy-boy on one of the numerous steamboats that cleaved the Mississippi. There he learned the first of two proficiencies — the art of gambling with cards and winning without resorting to common trickery.

The second accomplishment, his dexterity with a six-gun, followed when, tiring of riverboat life, he forsook its monotony, acquired a horse and gear, and headed West. He drifted for several years, and during that time the legend of his aptitude grew, and the cruel tag that men in their delight of the macabre hung upon him — the Widowmaker — came into usage. Aaron Ledbetter had sought none of it, but as is usually the way in such things, it came to pass.

Some called him a freak, declaring that his unbelievable ability with a pistol was due to a whim of nature, which had equipped him with somewhat short arms, slightly out of proportion to his six-foot height. Others termed him that rare phenomenon — a natural, a born killer, with all the lance-sharp components that make up the flawless gunman.

Whatever the cause he was without peer, and any who ever saw him in action frittered no time in doubt. But as could be expected he became a person apart, utterly alone, with every man an instinctive enemy and possible eventual opponent in a grim, ceaseless game of death.

Ledbetter was one year short of twenty-five that summer day when he paused at the foot of Capulin. He swung from the saddle, came to a stand beside the sorrel in that catlike coiled stance peculiar to him while he studied the oncoming riders.

None was familiar at that distance. He waited another full minute while he eased his tired muscles, and then, sighing, got back onto the horse. He'd best find out what it was all about. He'd be damned if he was going to have them dogging his

9

heels all the way to El Paso.

Brushing at the sweat accumulating on his forehead, he glanced around. Thing to do was take a little sashay off on a side trail and see if they followed. If they didn't, all well and good; he could mark them off as harmless travelers also moving south, and forget it. If they did . . .

He allowed the thought to go unfinished while he stared at a faint smoke haze to the west. A town . . . Chacosa, most likely. It was around there somewhere in the short hills. Chacosa would be as good a place as any if the three riders were out for trouble.

Aaron rode on, his eyes reaching ahead, searching for a split in the road. A quarter mile later he picked it up, immediately veered onto it. A fairly well-defined cattle trail, it worked across the brow of a small knoll for a short distance and then abruptly dropped off into a deep, sandy arroyo.

Out of sight, Ledbetter spurred to gain a sizable lead, pointing for a clump of wind-tortured cedars well up on the slope of a second hill. The grade was steep, and by the time the sorrel had reached and swung in behind the tangled growth, he was lathered and blowing hard.

Hunched forward in the saddle, Aaron waited. Within a few minutes the men appeared, walking their horses briskly, eyes on the trail. Reaching the fork, they halted. One, a thickset individual, climbed stiffly from his mount, and bending low, studied the hoofprints in the dust. It wasn't necessary for Ledbetter to wait any longer to see if they took the turnoff; that they were trailing him was apparent.

Wheeling the sorrel about, he struck due west for the smoke haze, making no effort to conceal his movements; the problem was there, and Aaron Ledbetter was not the kind to dodge the inevitable.

Near the middle of the afternoon, with the sun harsh on his face, he reached the settlement and turned into the single main street that split Chacosa, a dull gray helter-skelter collection of weathered structures, into sprawling halves.

It was his first time in the town, but it looked no different from a hundred others he had visited during his wanderings across the West, and the attitude of the citizenry toward him would also be the same, he knew. His one hope on arriving in a new town was that he might go unrecognized, that he could pass as just another gambler pausing for a few hours of serious poker playing.

But as the years passed he came to accept such as a futile wish; there was always someone who had seen him somewhere — and then would come trouble. Today it was even more certain; the men trailing him would bring it with them, and a confrontation was unavoidable. It was a hell of a way to live, he thought, and morosely viewed the street.

D. Wylder, General Store . . . Cimarron Saloon . . . The Owl Cafe . . . Feather's Harness

& Gun Shop . . . The Capulin Hotel . . . City Jail & Marshal . . . The Castlerock, Saloon & Gambling . . . Dr. James Pheebus . . . a dozen more business houses and shops.

The Castlerock — it appeared to be the largest and most prosperous of the several saloons. As well go there . . . Touching the sorrel with spurs, he guided the red toward the hitching rack fronting the square, squat building.

He was conscious of faces turned toward him, some curiously, some questioningly, as he moved through the ankle-deep dust. To all he returned a steady cool look, asking neither for friendship nor for consideration, perhaps only for a measure of understanding; but if that was true, of such Aaron Ledbetter was unaware.

He reached the front of the Castlerock, slowed to permit a bearded man and his wife to cross before him, and then angled in to the rail. He would have preferred stabling the sorrel; the horse deserved rest and care out of the driving sunlight; but circumstances dictated his mount be in the open where it could be easily seen and he, accordingly, located.

Dismounting, Ledbetter looped the reins about the adzed aspen, paused to glance down the street. The bearded man, stiff and unbending in a hallelujah-shouting, righteous sort of way, was heading into the marshal's office. Aaron gave brief wonder as to what trouble could be his, and then dismissed the thought as he saw the three riders come into view at the end of the row of buildings.

He waited a few more seconds, then stepped up onto the porch of the Castlerock and crossed leisurely to the recently varnished batwings. Brushing them aside with a forearm, he entered the shadow-filled building. He paused again, allowed his eyes to adjust, and then strode in a direct line to the bar running along the opposing wall.

The quick lull in conversation among the dozen or so patrons scattered about the room resumed almost at once. The bartender, a neatly dressed young man probably not yet in his twenties, smiled at him.

"Yessir?"

"A bottle," Aaron said. "And a glass."

The bartender filled the order quickly. Ledbetter jerked his head at an empty table in a back corner. "I'll be there."

He turned away, barely hearing the man murmur a second *yessir,* and sat down facing the doorway. Pouring himself a generous drink, he tossed it off, sighed, and settled down to wait.

The respite was of short duration. Ledbetter saw the doors part to admit the three men. He studied them closely and with interest. One he recognized — a dark, sullen-faced gunman named Harry Cerba, said to be part Indian. The others — the slim, loose-jointed blond with boyish features and the squat, roundheaded man — were strangers.

Only they were far from strangers in the

abstract sense of the term; they were the self-appointed avengers with whom he had to come to grips many times in the past. They were of the ones who took it upon themselves to right what, in the confines of their own mind, they deemed an injury, an injustice, no matter what the prior circumstances or reasons for the altercation. All that mattered to them was vengeance, swift and conclusive.

They had spotted him now. He watched as they sidled up to the bar with exaggerated indifference and called for whiskey. They all downed two shots and then, as one, turned, hooked their elbows on the edge of the counter, and surveyed the room.

Ledbetter smiled faintly. Did they believe him unaware of their purpose? If so, they must think him a fool. Pushing back his chair to allow himself free arm movement, he reached down, grasped the worn handle of his pistol. The smooth curved surfaces, with the round indentations where he had inset on either side ten-dollar gold pieces as tokens of luck, felt cool and reassuring.

He fondled the heavy weapon briefly, lifted it halfway from its oiled holster, allowed it to drop back into place, sure now there were no encumbrances that might hinder or delay its use even for the smallest fraction of a second.

At that moment the squat one of the three pushed himself away from the bar, wheeled around slowly. Flanked by Cerba and the blond, he moved toward Aaron's table.

There was no visible change in Ledbetter. He watched the men approach with cool unconcern, but beneath that facade he was swiftly marshaling the forces that had seen him through two dozen or more occasions of a similar nature.

The men halted, the squat one a step to the fore. Ledbetter, his long lips a tight line, considered them in contemptuous silence, and then finally spoke.

"Seems you caught up — after two days. What's it all about?"

The squat man seemed taken aback momentarily. "You know goddamned well what it's all about!" he shouted, recovering.

Ledbetter, left hand toying with his empty glass, merely stared.

"Name's Rosen," the man continued, his eyes bright with anger. "That mean anything to you?"

Aaron continued to twirl the glass, made no reply.

"Was my brother you gunned down in Monument!"

Cynicism tugged at the corners of Ledbetter's mouth. "And you swore on his dead body you'd hunt me down, even the score."

"Said I would — and I mean just that —"

"Figured that was it," Ledbetter cut in wearily, signaling to the bartender for more glasses. "Sit down, have another drink. . . . Like as not it'll be your last."

2

Town marshal Sam Back did not note the arrival of Aaron Ledbetter, nor did he see the three men who trailed him into Chacosa. He was slumped in his aged swivel chair, booted feet propped upon his desk, while he brooded gloomily over the past.

No one remembered it but this day — this very day — marked the beginning of his twentieth year as Chacosa's lawman. Nineteen years on the job! Nineteen years of faithful service — and what did they care? Not a whit. He could fall dead in that stinking office and it would maybe be weeks before anyone missed him and dropped by to see what had happened.

He sighed wistfully. It hadn't always been that way. Once they had looked up to Sam Back, had respected him for the tough, hard-nosed lawman that he was . . . *or had been.* He sat up a bit straighter as that thought trickled through his mind.

After a moment he stirred impatiently. Well, maybe he was sixty years old — that didn't mean he still wasn't a good lawman. They didn't *know* he wasn't — they just went ahead and assumed that because he was sixty, and had been around for a long time, he was a has-been.

Hell, he was a better man today than most of the young squirts strutting around wearing a badge! Ask any of the old heads — the ranchers and the stagecoach drivers, even some of the government men who'd worked the Territories a few years ago — they'd tell you mighty quick that Sam Back was one of the best.

There were plenty who'd remember the time he, single-handed, broke up that rustling bunch down near Abilene. And that killer — what was his name — the one who shot up Rimrock Junction; who was it that tracked him for four days and nights and finally brought him down? Sam Back, that's who.

And there was that gang from up north, Miles City it was, who thought they were going to take over Waco, jar, jug and candy case. He'd been only a deputy then, but that hadn't stopped him; he'd waded right in, tamed that bunch, and damn quick put things back in proper order.

But folks forgot those things, forgot a lot of things. And they expected too much. Pete Vedic was a good example. Sure Pete was an outlaw and he and his bunch were holed up no more than twenty-five miles back in the hills, but he wasn't bothering anybody around Chacosa.

So why should some of them be worrying about Pete Vedic? Long as he stayed clear of the town, left the ranchers alone, there was no reason starting a war with him. He guessed there were a few who thought he was afraid of Vedic, that he was doing everything possible to avoid the outlaw.

Wasn't nothing to that! Sam Back knuckled under to no man. It was simply that there was no need, no reason. And a man was a plain fool to stir up a den of sleeping snakes. Long as Vedic stayed at Devil's Creek and didn't come into Chacosa, there was no point in looking for trouble.

He wondered if people ever gave thought that Vedic, possibly, was leaving Chacosa alone because Sam Back was the law there. Personally, he didn't know Vedic, but it could be the outlaw knew him — and accordingly was strictly avoiding the town. Did folks ever think of that? Seems they always —

The old lawman's meandering, bitter thoughts came to a stop as the solid beat of boot heels sounded on the landing outside the door. He looked up, frowned deeply as Everett Feak, followed by his wife Jenny, stamped into the dusty office.

Feak had a small ranch a few miles north of town, a dry, starve-out spread that never had done much good. It was in direct contrast to the place of Ev's brother, Carter, who had the largest and most prosperous ranch in the county.

Ev appeared drawn and worried. Back dropped his feet to the floor, squared himself around.

"Howdy, Ev, Jenny. Trouble?"

Something important, he hoped, and not a

piddling bellyache about Tom Seever's dog or the like. Maybe somebody'd run off with the church's money. Ev and Jenny were big workers in the church.

Feak clawed at his beard agitatedly. "Sam, we're needing your help real bad."

"What I'm here for," the lawman said crisply. "What's it all about?"

"It's my — our daughter — Melanie. . . ."

The marshal nodded slowly. Likely the girl had run off with one of the hired hands — or maybe even some worthless drummer. Was to be expected, strict as they were with her. Hell, she must be sixteen or seventeen now, and far as he knew she'd never been allowed even to look at a man.

"What about her?"

"Been kidnapped."

Jenny Feak moved to a chair, sat down limply, and began to sob. Sam Back got to his feet, disbelief on his weathered features.

"Kidnapped!" he echoed. "You sure? How do you know?"

"This's how," Feak said, and reaching into his pocket, produced a folded sheet of paper. Handing it to Back, he said: "Got this yesterday morning."

"Took your time bringing it to me," Sam muttered, sitting down. He unfolded the sheet, smoothed its creases. "How long's the girl been gone?"

"Tuesday."

19

"And this here's Thursday. How's it happen you're just now telling me about it?"

The lawman was nettled. Everett Feak nodded humbly. "Weren't too sure what'd happened to her. . . . Was late Tuesday, anyway."

Simmering, Sam leaned over the note, began to read. Written in pencil on the reverse side of a circular advertising Hall's Sicilian Hair Renewer, it was brief and to the point.

Feak:
I got your daughter. Five thousand dollars buys her back.
This man will meet you at Bear Paw Crossing nine a.m. Friday.
Bring cash in paper and coin. Don't give it to nobody but this man.
Keep the U. S. Marshal out of this if you want to see her alive again.

A Friend

Sam Back stiffened with anger. The note had warned against bringing in a government lawman, hadn't mentioned him. Apparently he counted for nothing. Masking his irritation, he continued to study the note.

"Any idea who this — this friend is?"

"Pete Vedic," Feak said readily.

The marshal looked up in surprise. "Now, what makes you so sure of that?"

"Fellow that brought the note, he told me," Feak answered, mopping at his face. "Said Vedic

20

meant business, that I'd better raise the money — or else."

Sam Back considered that. "Expect he does. What're you aiming to do?"

"Do?" the rancher said in a strangled voice. "Raise the money — that's what! Don't know how but I've just got to!"

The old lawman nodded sympathetically, studied the quietly sobbing Jenny Feak. "How you figure I can help? If you're aiming to pay, ain't no need for the law."

"Realize that, but it's put us between a rock and a hard place. Was wondering if you'd go with me to the bank, do some talking up for me."

"Think Harvey'll lend you the money?"

"Don't rightly know. Place of mine's mortgaged to the hilt, but I've got to get five thousand somewheres. . . . When I think of Melly in the hands of them renegades. . . . She's just a girl, Sam — a little girl —"

"Now, don't get yourself all worked up," Back said gently, reaching for his hat. "We'll find us a way. What about your brother?"

Ev listened to his wife's weeping for a moment, then shook his head. "Hoping it won't come to that — considering how things stand between us."

The old lawman settled his flat-crowned headpiece squarely over his eyes, brushed the stray white locks of hair to the nape of his neck. "Know you ain't exactly on the best of terms with Carter, but time can come when a man has to swallow his pride. However, let's have us a little talk with Harvey first."

The rancher bobbed his head numbly. Turning to his wife, he said, "No use in your coming, Mother. Wait here."

Jenny Feak stirred, removed her handkerchief from her eyes to signify understanding. Sam Back, the old almost forgotten sense of self-assurance strongly asserting itself within him, crossed the room and stepped out into the wilting sunlight. Feak hurried to catch up, and together they walked to the bank and entered.

Harvey Kitchell, graying, well dressed and soberly businesslike, glanced up from his desk in the corner. Except for Augie Finesilver in the teller's cage, the place was deserted.

"Harvey," Back said, coming straight to the point, "Ev's got a serious problem and needs help. Both our help."

Kitchell leaned forward slightly on his elbows. "Always glad to assist when I can," he said cautiously.

"Well, here's your chance. Ev's got to have five thousand dollars — in cash."

The banker's eyes flickered. "You say five thousand dollars?"

"What I said," the lawman replied, and placed the ransom note on the desk. "Here's the reason."

Harvey Kitchell scanned the paper hurriedly, read it a second time. After a moment he began to shake his head.

"Terrible thing . . . and I'm sorry about it, Ev. Wish I could help, but you know how things stand. If your place was clear —"

The rancher stirred helplessly, and his voice took on a note of desperation. "Realize all that, Harvey, but you can see the fix I'm in! Just got to raise that money somehow — somewhere. Ain't there nothing you can do, no way —"

"What about your brother? Maybe Carter will lend it to you."

"I — I don't know —"

"You know how things stand between them," Sam Back cut in. "Reason we came to you."

Kitchell shrugged. "But at a time like this —"

"Way Carter feels about money, doubt if it'll make much difference. You think he'll care a rap whether Ev's daughter gets hurt or not?"

"He might," Kitchell said mildly. "Worth finding out."

Abruptly Feak spun, and carefully holding his face from the two men, strode to the window. Sam studied the rancher's bowed figure for a time, and then brought his attention again to the banker.

"Not right to turn him down cold like that, Harvey. His own flesh and blood he's buying back."

Kitchell frowned. "I'd like to help him, Marshal. Honestly would — but it just can't be done. Man with no more assets than he can show — and not much of a future —"

"Well, I aim to help him," Sam said, "and I got

a scheme worked out that'll do the trick. Be needing your cooperation, however."

Kitchell made no comment, simply waited.

"Want you to lend Ev that money, let him take it to Pete Vedic and get the girl —"

"Pete Vedic?" the banker said, half rising. "That who kidnapped her?"

"He's the one . . . . Now, I —"

Harvey Kitchell began to shake his head. The old lawman, suddenly angry, reached out and pushed him back into his chair.

"Hear me out, goddamnit! You let him have the cash just long enough to ransom the girl. While he's turning over the money, me and a dozen men'll be hiding out in the brush. Soon as I see the girl's in the clear, I'll give the word and we'll close in, nab the man Vedic sent to pick up the money, and get him and your five thousand dollars, too."

Kitchell stared at the lawman with fathomless eyes. From his place at the window Feak had half turned, a hopeful look on his face.

"Be me personally guaranteeing you'll get the money back," the marshal, heartened by the banker's silence, rushed on. "And we'll just be borrowing it for two, three hours — four, at the most."

Kitchell's shoulders lifted, fell. "Plan like that just might work, Sam, only —"

"Only what?"

"Where'd you get a dozen men — or even a half a dozen willing to tangle with Vedic's bunch? No, if it was —"

Back's florid features darkened as temper drove through him in a sudden gust. "If it was somebody heading up the posse besides me — that what you mean? You figure I'm too old to pull it off, that I can't handle —"

Kitchell raised his hand. "Now, I never said that, Marshal, but since you brought it up yourself, maybe a younger lawman could do it."

"But not me. Say it out flat, Harvey."

The banker shook his head. "Won't argue with you. No point." Deliberately he shifted his glance to Feak. "I'm sorry, Ev. Wish there was something I could do."

"Forget it," the lawman said before the rancher could shape a reply. "You're like all the rest of the folks around here — figure I'm no good anymore except to handle the Saturday night drunks. But you're wrong, plenty wrong — and I aim to prove it!"

He wheeled stiffly, started for the door. "Come on, Ev," he said as he drew near the rancher. "Let's get out of here. Place has got a bad smell."

Rigid, with Feak following numbly, he walked into the open. Outside, the rancher caught at his arm, stayed him.

"Sam — I —"

Eyes glowing, inflamed by anger and indignation, the old lawman faced his friend.

"Maybe you better go talk to your brother," he said. "Up to you whether you pay off or not —

25

but I'm promising you this, Ev, money or not I'm moving in on this thing. Ain't no two-bit outlaw going to fool around with none of my people!"

Everett Feak frowned, taken back by the hard rush of words. "That mean you —"

"Means I'll get your daughter back for you, safe and sound, and bust this Vedic gang wide open while I'm doing it!"

3

Rosen advanced to the chair directly opposite Ledbetter and sat down warily. Aaron could see the resemblance now to the man who had called him out in Monument City. This Rosen would be the older, however.

Harry Cerba, his dark face inscrutable, his movements smooth, unhurried, took the seat to Rosen's left, the shambling blond to his right. The young bartender scurried up with three more glasses, scurried away.

"Keep your hands on the table," Ledbetter said quietly, and began to pour from the bottle.

Rosen's color deepened. He swallowed hard. "Don't you go trying nothing," he muttered.

Aaron shrugged, set the bottle aside. "For a man who's got the odds with him, you're plenty jumpy. . . . Drink up."

Rosen's fingers trembled as they encircled his glass. "Reckon I've got reasons not to trust you none."

Ledbetter studied his drink briefly, took a sip. "Put it this way — you think you have. There's a hell of a big difference."

The conversation was unnerving Rosen, breaking him down. Evidently it was the first time he had faced a man with the thought of killing in his mind. Sympathy moved through Ledbetter and then, as abruptly, he washed it away; a pistol in the hands of a nervous, frightened man could kill just as surely as one held by the deadliest gunman. He touched the two other with his eyes.

"Always like to know who I'm up against. Remember Cerba. Who's the kid?"

Rosen gulped his drink, placed his empty glass on the table, bottom up. "Name's Tucker — and he ain't no kid."

Aaron nodded, deliberately pleasant, to the blond, who only stared at him silently. Elsewhere in the Castlerock a hush had fallen. The promise of violence hung like a thick cloud over the room, and all who were there waited and watched with a breathless sort of fascination.

Tucker and Cerba finished their drinks, and like Rosen, reversed their glasses. Ledbetter took note, refilled his own. Leaving it untouched, he settled his flat gaze on Rosen.

"You know what you're doing?"

Rosen bobbed his head slowly. "And I figure I'll be doing the country a big favor — something somebody ought've done a long time ago."

"Maybe you think so," Aaron said coldly. "Like a lot of others, you don't know all —"

"Know enough!" Rosen blurted. "Know you gunned down my brother, left his family to shift for themselves. . . . Ought to be proud of yourself, mister — proud of what you done! That Widowmaker name they hung on you sure fits!"

A murmur of surprise rippled through the crowd in the saloon. Ledbetter's eyes narrowed, and for the first time anger plucked at his features.

"Your brother got what he asked for. I wasn't looking for trouble, but he forced the issue."

Tucker laughed, a high-pitched cackle. "You're trying to make it sound like you need a reason to draw on a man."

"Never used a gun yet unless I was pushed into it," Aaron said.

The Tuckers were plentiful. He had seen them everywhere — always in the background, safe, egging others on while they avidly awaited bloodshed with a morbid anticipation. More often than not it was the Tuckers of the world who made it necessary for men like him to use a gun in order to stay alive.

"Sure, sure," Harry Cerba said, breaking his silence. "I'm bleeding for you. . . . That gambler in Dodge, he was pushing real hard."

"Don't feel called on to explain to you," Ledbetter replied in the same even tone, "but that gambler was dealing from his sleeve. I called him on it. He went for a pistol."

"All this talking — it don't mean nothing to me!" Rosen exclaimed suddenly. He was sweating profusely and there was a nervousness to his manner. "Trailed you all the way from Monument for one thing — square up for my brother. Brought some help because I'm smart enough to know I can't do it alone —"

"Anytime you're ready," Ledbetter said softly.

Rosen's lips parted and his eyes seemed to sink deeper into his round face. "I'll pick the time —"

"The time's now," Aaron said. "You've already picked it."

Rosen swallowed hard, glanced uncertainly toward Harry Cerba. It was as if he were having second thoughts about the matter and was discovering he had no stomach for the situation he had created. The dark-faced gunman nodded. Trapped, Rosen shook his head.

"This is going to be my way. Aim to kill you, one way or another."

Ledbetter shrugged. "You've made it plain. Reckon I ought to say I'm sorry for your family."

"Ain't got no family — only my brother's wife — widow, and their three kids."

"Sorry for them, then. Why don't you forget this?"

"No, sir — not a chance!"

"Brother of yours isn't worth it. He was a fool, trying to make himself look good in front of a saloon crowd."

"He was still my kin — and you could've walked away."

"Tried, but he wouldn't let it drop."

"You could've handled him. He wasn't much more'n a kid, barely twenty."

"A kid with a gun," Ledbetter corrected, "and itching to use it. Let's get on with it."

Rosen's color drained. Tucker stirred uneasily

on his chair. Only Harry Cerba, his sullen face immobile, seemed unperturbed. Cerba was an old head at the game; he took things as they came. Over to Aaron's right the Castlerock's swamper, an elderly man in stained, patched overalls, ceased his sweeping, leaned on his broom.

"I'll say it once more," Ledbetter said. "Get up slow — all of you. Keep your hands away from your guns, and walk out of here. That'll end it."

There was only silence. Rosen stared at Aaron with bright, fixed eyes. Suddenly he sprang erect.

"No!" he shouted, and reached for his pistol.

In that same instant, it seemed, he staggered back, began to crumple as a broad stain appeared magically on his chest. Tucker spun half around, dead before he could rise. Harry Cerba, the last to die, managed to clear his holster, but he failed even to bring his weapon above the table's top.

A yell went up as smoke boiled through the shocking echoes that filled the room. Cerba toppled sideways. Reflex action triggered his pistol. Its report crashed, arousing a new chain of sound, and over near the wall the old swamper gasped and sank to the floor.

"My God!" someone moaned in an awed voice as a hush settled in.

It had all happened so fast that it threw a paralysis upon the onlookers in the saloon. Ledbetter

31

had scarcely moved — yet he was half out of his chair, pistol sticking straight out from his body, arm clamped tight to his side. It was unbelievable.

The mass stupefaction broke. A man edged over to the swamper, knelt, turned him over on his back. He glanced up. "Right through the heart."

No one bothered to check the three men strewn before Ledbetter's table, and all cast only covert glances at him, seemingly unwilling to meet his hard, splintery gaze straight on. After a moment the rigidity of his lean shape lessened and he drew himself fully upright. The square line of his shoulders gave way and he looked down, a deep sigh escaping his lips.

Immediately a man at the bar removed his hat, mopped vigorously at his balding head. "Ain't never seen the beat of it!" he said in a hoarse, subdued voice. "All of them just setting there — like they was talking business or something. . . . Next thing three of 'em dead — four, counting Amos."

"Didn't even see him draw that gun — and I was looking right at him!" another commented.

"Dead — killed three of them — *three men!*" someone else said in a disbelieving, shocked way.

The bartender, despite his youth, was the first to recover his equanimity. "Somebody," he said, "ought to fetch the marshal."

Everyone's glance shifted immediately to Ledbetter, at the moment punching out the empty shell casings in his pistol and reloading with fresh cartridges. He looked up, nodded.

"Sure. Get the marshal."

4

Sam Back watched Feak and his wife move off into the street, and swore deeply. Why the hell did he have to open his mouth and say he'd take care of everything — for them not to worry, he'd recover their daughter for them?

They hadn't really asked him to do it; they had only come to him for advice maybe; but somehow matters had gotten all fired up — possibly because of Harvey Kitchell's attitude toward him — and the next thing he knew he was making a lot of big promises.

Promises he was pretty sure he couldn't keep, for he hadn't the vaguest notion what could be done. He sure couldn't go barging into Pete Vedic's camp at Devil's Creek and demand the outlaws turn Melly Feak over to him; they'd laugh in his face — and he'd be lucky if that was all they did.

And he'd get no help from the outside; few if any of the local men, when they learned it was Pete Vedic and his crowd they'd be up against, would join a posse. And as for the government lawmen, who knew where one could be found at that precise moment?

He gave the Army thought. There were soldiers at Fort Union. Hope rose within him, and quickly ebbed. Getting troops to Chacosa would require days, and time, thanks to Ev Feak, had about run out.

He swore again, wheeled to his desk, and plumped down into the chair. If only he'd kept his head, not been so goddamned anxious to prove to everybody that he was still a good lawman, he wouldn't be in such a tight corner. Now, when this blew over, things would be even worse —

He sat up straight. Three gunshots, so closely spaced they sounded as one, and then a fourth, broke the afternoon quiet. The lawman remained motionless, startled by the unfamiliar reports. It had been a long time since there was a shooting in Chacosa. A shooting! Abruptly he leaped to his feet, galvanized by the realization of what was taking place.

Jamming his hat on his head, he snatched up the double-barreled shotgun gathering dust in a corner, and rushed into the street. Several men were trotting toward the Castlerock Saloon. Taking his cue from them, he followed.

He reached the porch, elbowed his way into the knot of curious clustered around the doors. "One side," he said briskly. "One side."

The group parted reluctantly, and Sam Back halted just short of the batwings. Not certain what to expect, he checked the loads in the shotgun, and then, feeling the push of eyes on him, stepped carefully into the saloon.

The odor of burnt gunpowder and layers of

smoke still hung in the poorly lit room. He saw first the stunned look on the faces of the men at the bar — and then he caught sight of the dead. Three men near a table in the corner; another — Amos Greene, the Castlerock's swamper — over close to the wall. In the following moment he saw Aaron Ledbetter.

The tall gunman-gambler was leaning against one of the ceiling supports, a drink in his hand. Sam felt the man's diamond-hard eyes probing him.

Experience had long ago taught the lawman the necessity for never showing indecision and fear, regardless of the situation. Holding the shotgun in the crook of his arm, he strode unhesitatingly into the center of the room.

"Just what's going on here?" he demanded, glancing around.

A dozen men began to speak at once. The marshal shook his head, lifted a hand for silence. "Maybe it'd be better was I to just ask some questions." Singling out a short individual near the end of the counter, he said: "You see it, Otey?"

"Sure did," the man replied, taking a step forward. "Was right here from the start."

"Who done the killings?" It was apparent to Sam Back the man near the table had been the one, but it was always best to proceed in an orderly, businesslike manner.

Otey looked at Ledbetter, nodded cautiously. "Was him. . . . They — one of them dead ones called him the Widowmaker."

Judas Priest — the Widowmaker! Right here in his own town! Sam Back felt his lower jaw sag. Hastily, he recovered himself.

"How'd it happen?"

Otey cast a second glance at Ledbetter, and then, shrugging, said, "Well, he come in first, got hisself a bottle, and set down at that table in the corner there. Pretty soon in come them three."

"They was looking for trouble, Marshal," a man farther along the bar volunteered. "Could easy see that."

Otey paused impatiently. Sam nodded, said, "Go ahead."

"Well, he invited them to set down, have a drink. Maybe their last one, he told them —"

The lawman lifted his hand, frowned. "You actually hear him say that — them same words, I mean?"

"Yes, sir," Otey replied, and glanced along the bar for verification. Several others had overheard the remark.

Sam Back said, "Then what?"

"They all set down, and everything was going along nice as you please, when all of a sudden the one in the middle there jumps up and grabs for his gun. The two others done the same — only none of them ever got to pull a trigger because they was dead. Mean that, Marshal. It was just that quick."

Sam Back was no stranger to the talents of

Aaron Ledbetter, and he doubted none of what Otey had told him. But deep within his mind something was beginning to stir; *the Widow-maker — the notorious, dreaded killer standing right there before him. If there was only some way —* Eyes narrowing, he allowed his thoughts to rush on unchecked while he pointed to Amos Greene.

"Him?"

"Stray bullet. When that Indian-looking jasper fell over his gun went off. Hit Amos."

"Was a clear case of self-defense, Marshal," the bartender said, fingering his bow tie. "Every man here'll testify to that."

The idea struggling for life in the old lawman's subconscious rose to the surface in that exact instant, heaven-sent, crystal clear — and desperate in character. But it could work, and if it did all the lost, sedentary years would be wiped out in a single act; he would again be a lawman of consequence. He came to an affirmative decision, willing to gamble on anything.

"No doubt," he said coldly to the younger man. Moving slowly, he crossed to where he was opposite the table from Ledbetter. "I'm Sam Back, town marshal."

Aaron frowned. "Thought I'd heard somewhere you were dead —"

"Back — goddamn it — not Bass!" the lawman snapped, irritated as always by the all-too-frequent error.

Ledbetter shifted his shoulders, realizing he'd pricked a nerve. "Sorry," he murmured. "Sorry about this shooting, too. Tried to talk them out of it."

"Expect you did."

"Don't go blaming him," one of the patrons broke in. "He's telling you straight. Tried his best to keep them from starting something."

"For a fact, Sam. Just wasn't nothing he could do. We all seen that."

Otey moved out a few paces, looked down at the dead men. "Don't look like much. Outlaws, I suspect — so there ain't no harm done. Always heard this here Widowmaker never killed no man what didn't need killing."

Sam listened patiently. He watched Aaron place his empty glass on the table.

"I've heard of you, too," he said, shifting the shotgun slightly. "Seems your regular name's Ledbetter."

"Prefer that to the other."

"Can't say as I fault you. You know these men?"

"One of them — the Indian — is Harry Cerba. Other two I just met today. Been trailing me."

A slyness crept into Sam Back's eyes. "Trailing you from where?"

"Monument City."

"Why?"

Ledbetter shifted on his feet. "Little trouble with the brother of one. Name of Rosen."

"Trouble. Reckon that means you shot him down."

"In a fair fight — yes."

"And this brother and his two *compadres* were out to get even, that so?"

Aaron Ledbetter nodded. "About the size of it," he said patiently.

Sam Back drew himself up fully, his features stern. "And knowing this," he said in a clear, distinct voice, "knowing things would end in gunplay, you led them right into my town!"

"I didn't know for sure what they wanted until they came here."

"Maybe — but I figure you had a right good idea."

Ledbetter again shifted his weight. Lawmen were different. In some towns there would have been no questions asked. Witnesses would have cleared him, just as they had here in Chacosa, and that would have ended it — except he was usually asked to leave immediately. He was a bit puzzled by Sam Back, however; it was as if the old lawman was trying to build something against him — work up a case.

"I ain't thanking you none for bringing this hell raising here," the marshal said. "You can see what it's done — got one of our local folks killed."

"Wasn't him that did it," Otey protested. "Was a stray bullet from the Indian's gun — like I told you!"

"And I heard you — but dead's dead, and if he hadn't come here, bringing trouble, Amos'd be alive. So —" Abruptly Sam Back's shotgun swung up, its twin barrels only inches from

40

Aaron Ledbetter's belly, its tall, curved hammers pulled to full cocked position. "So I reckon you'd better come along with me, Mister Widowmaker."

In the sudden hush Ledbetter stiffened as his features changed slowly to ice. But he was no fool. Hands motionless, he stared at the lawman.

"Why?" he asked quietly.

"Ain't sure, but I figure I got good reason. You coming here, bringing them three hardcases with you — and causing the death of an innocent man."

"You heard what's been said. Wasn't my gun that killed him."

"Know it wasn't, but way I look at it, you're responsible. Had no business coming here. . . . Now, raise your hands up — high."

Ledbetter lifted his arms. Cautious, Sam Back circled the table, leaned forward, and lifting the pistol from Aaron's holster, thrust it under his own waistband.

"That's right," he murmured. "Just you play it smart and there'll be no more shooting." He ducked his head at the doors. "Move out. We're taking a little walk to the jail."

"Hell, Sam, you can't do that!" a well-dressed man standing next to Otey declared. "Ain't right!"

"Ain't right that Amos is dead, either," the lawman said. "And somebody's going to pay for it. Now, all of you stand aside and keep out of this. I know my job and I'm taking care of it."

5

Ledbetter, grimly silent, with Sam Back following closely, crossed to the batwing doors and entered the street. Men gathered on the Castlerock's porch and along the sidewalk drew aside, gave them ample room. Several questions were hurled at the old lawman, but he merely shook his head.

They reached the jail. Ledbetter paused on the landing, anger mounting steadily within him. Sam Back pressed the muzzle of his shotgun against the tall man's spine. Ledbetter half turned.

"Take that goddamned thing out of my back," he said softly.

The lawman withdrew his weapon a few inches, glanced over his shoulder to the Castlerock, where a crowd was forming.

"Get inside," he said urgently.

Aaron stepped into the stuffy confines of the small office, again paused.

"First cell," the marshal said. "Hurry it up!"

Ledbetter entered the cage. Immediately Sam Back clanged the grille door shut, turned the lock, and tossed the keys onto his desk. Wheeling, he retraced his steps to the door. The crowd that had been shaping up in front of the saloon was now gathering in the street before the jail.

"You really aim to try him for Amos Greene's death?" a voice asked.

"I'm holding him," the marshal said, cradling the shotgun in his arms. "Ain't saying no more'n that."

"But how can you —"

"Long as I'm the law around here, things are going to be run right," Sam Back said. "Now, I want you to move on, get about your business — and leave me to mine."

Abruptly he stepped back into the room, and despite the withering heat, kicked the door closed. That done, he sighed heavily, and releasing the hammers on the scattergun, stood it in its customary place.

He'd been playing a dangerous game, shepherding a man of the Widowmaker's caliber along the street even for so short a distance. He was glad it was over. Ledbetter could have made it tough. For a moment he stood in the center of the room, staring at the floor while he assembled his thoughts. Then, reaching for a chair, he dragged it up close to the cell where the gunman was imprisoned, and settled himself.

Immediately Ledbetter, his voice still low and threaded with that quality of controlled wrath, said, "What's this all about?"

Sam struggled to remain casual. "Told you what the charge was — bringing a shoot-out into my town, getting an innocent man killed."

"Can't hold me for that."

"Held prisoners for less, but if you've got to have a charge, disturbing the peace'll do."

Aaron Ledbetter sat down on the hard cot, swore in exasperation. It was a legitimate charge, he guessed, even if pretty far-fetched. It would cost him a few days, possibly a fine. He glanced at Sam Back. Maybe that was the key; maybe that was what the lawman was interested in.

"How much will it cost me to get out?"

The marshal wagged his head. "Have to wait for the judge. Be here in maybe a couple of weeks. Anyway, that ain't the point."

Ledbetter's features were bleak. "What is the point?"

Sam Back steadied himself. He leaned forward. "How many killings you got to your credit now, mister? Eighteen? Nineteen? Or maybe it's twenty. Just how many?"

"Seems you're keeping the score — not me."

"Anyway, it's a God-awful plenty, and something that sets a man to shaking when he thinks on it. Ain't hard to understand why they call you the Widowmaker."

"Never gunned a man down unless he forced me into it."

"No, 'course not. But a reputation like yours draws trouble like honey brings the flies."

"Hardly blame me for that. I don't ask for it."

"Maybe not, but you're overlooking one thing; reputation like you've got don't just grow

44

the way a man grows hair. Had to be something start it."

Aaron said nothing. Sam glanced toward the street as if to assure himself they were alone, and then, satisfied, continued.

"It'll keep growing, too, and you'll go right on killing. Oh, sure, it'll be self-defense. I ain't saying it won't always be self-defense — but the fact is it'll really be murder, because no man stands a chance drawing against you." The old lawman paused, cocked his head to one side. "So what's the answer?"

"You tell me," Ledbetter said, shrugging wearily.

"Put you out of business, that's what. Just plain get you out of the way."

Aaron studied the lawman narrowly. "On a charge of disturbing the peace? In case you don't know it, Marshal, the law sets the punishment for crimes, and there's a maximum —"

"Seems you know all about the law."

"I've been up before — and in bigger towns than yours."

"But maybe this is where you're going to trip up — a little one-horse burg called Chacosa."

Sam Back rose, stalked to the window, and looked into the street while he allowed his words to have their full impact. He remained there a full minute, a starched figure in gray corded pants tucked neatly into knee-high flat-heeled boots, and white shirt with black string tie. Against the sunlight's glare his snowy hair and mustache contrasted sharply against a florid skin.

Ledbetter made no reply, refusing to contest the statement. Finally the lawman wheeled, resumed his chair.

"Way things stand with you, there ain't a wanted dodger out on you anywhere in the country because you're smart enough to keep your nose clean. You always fix it so there's witnesses who'll swear you done your killing in self-defense. That's why you let them three men track you here to my town. Wanted to be sure people'd know it was self-defense. . . ."

"There anything wrong in that?"

"Maybe not, but thing I'm getting at is you're dodging the letter of the law — and there ain't a lawman west of the Missouri who wouldn't sell his soul to the devil if he could get something on you. . . . And there ain't a judge living who wouldn't part with his right arm for a chance to put you behind bars for good."

"Takes a charge —"

"And I figure I've got one," Sam Back said, his voice rising triumphantly. "Bringing violence into a peaceful town, creating a disturbance that brought about the murder of an innocent man — putting a lot of other folks in danger. Mister, I can nail you down good, and you know why? Because, like I said, the law's been looking for a way to get you for a long time — for just an excuse. . . . And I got it."

Ledbetter's eyes had pulled down into narrower slits. "No trumped-up deal like that —"

"Ain't trumped up at all. There's a local citizen dead. Can't get around that. Maybe no judge'll be able to hang you for it, but I'm betting he'll give you a few years in the pen — especially when I get through laying the facts before him."

Aaron studied the older man's face closely. He supposed there was some truth, some foundation to what the lawman was saying, and if he were hauled into court there was little doubt the cards would be stacked against him because of the past. But the whole thing had a smell to it, and he hadn't missed the sly glances the lawman had continually thrown at him during his windy oration.

"All right, Marshal," he said, taking a wild shot. "You've told me where I stand. What're you getting down to?"

Sam Back nodded crisply, rose again, checked the street. Finding it empty, he faced Ledbetter.

"Matter of fact, happens to be a way we can clear all this up."

Aaron smiled dryly. "What I figured. Now, get this straight — I'm no hired gun."

"Not asking you to be. Just in bad need of a little favor."

Ledbetter settled back. "I'm listening."

The lawman cleared his throat. "Been a girl by the name of Melanie Feak kidnapped. Couple days ago. Ransom's five thousand dollars. Her pa's got a little outfit north of here and I doubt if the whole shebang's worth that much money, so you can see there ain't hardly a chance of him paying off unless he can borrow the money from somewheres."

"So?"

"You know an outlaw name of Pete Vedic?"

"Met him once or twice."

"He's the one who grabbed her. Sent the ransom note to her pa by one of his bunch. They're holed up in an old mining town about twenty-five miles west of here."

"Get yourself a posse, root them out."

Sam Back hesitated. "Not that easy. Place is like a fort, and posses are hard to raise. Besides, what'd happen to the girl while we was doing it? Only a kid, sixteen, maybe seventeen."

"Probably nothing that hasn't already happened to her. Where do I come in?"

"Want you to go there, bring her back."

Ledbetter came off the cot in a single move. "What?"

"You could do it — easy. Nobody else could get in the camp, but they'd let you. You're their kind — no offense, understand — so there'd be no trouble."

"Doubt that. They'd treat any outsider the same."

"Don't think so. All you'd need say was you're riding through, want to lay over for the night. Far as you know Devil's Creek's still booming and you're maybe looking for a game. Vedic'll believe what you say. Then, once you're there, you can figure a way to get the girl and pull out."

"Can see you don't know Pete Vedic," Ledbetter said.

"Never seen the man, but it'd be a cinch for you. Probably even be glad you come by."

"Not likely," Aaron replied, shaking his head. "Expect my chances would be a lot better facing up to those charges you've —"

"I'm guaranteeing you right now they wouldn't," the lawman broke in. "I'll see to it — I'll have the backing of every sheriff and town marshal in the country to help me make them stick. Likely be a few who'll even be willing to stretch the truth a mite."

Ledbetter stirred impatiently. "This girl, she something special to you?"

"Nope. Hardly know her, but I can't let Vedic get away with something like this and I — well — folks around here don't figure . . ."

The lawman's voice faded. Aaron considered him in silence, searched for the words left unspoken. After a moment he nodded.

"This whole thing wouldn't have something to do with your reputation, would it, Marshal? They've got you pegged a has-been and you're maybe out to prove them all wrong? That it?"

Sam Back stiffened with anger. "No such a goddamn thing! Just giving you a chance to square yourself — and either you take it or squat right there on that cot and wait until the judge shows up."

"Blackmail —"

"Don't figure it that way myself. Just happens you're in position to do me — the town — a big favor. I'm giving you the chance."

"Still blackmail, Marshal, and you know it."

"All right, goddamn it!" Sam Back said explosively. "It's blackmail. What's your answer?"

Aaron Ledbetter brushed at the sweat on his forehead, envisioned days, perhaps weeks cooped up in a cell while he awaited the arrival of the circuit judge. He weighed that against the possibility of getting into Pete Vedic's outlaw nest — and getting out with the girl, both alive.

The odds would be short, but at least he'd be free and not sweating out the days in an iron cage. And who knew what a judge might do? It was just possible old Sam Back, supported by a bunch of overzealous lawmen, could make something stick.

"All right," he said. "You've got a deal."

6

Sam Back sighed gustily. "Being smart, Ledbetter. Wasn't joshing you none. I'd've done my damndest to put you in the pen if you hadn't seen things my way."

Aaron said nothing. The lawman rose, got the keys, and stepped up to the iron door. He hesitated, peered through the bars.

"One thing — you ain't thinking of pulling out —" Ledbetter said: "Only guarantee you'll get is my word."

"All I'm asking for. You giving it?"

"I am."

"Good enough," Back said, and unlocked the grille.

He stepped back, smiling. "Howsomever, reckon it's only right to warn you — just in case it slips your mind — I'll have wanted dodgers out for you from here to Memphis if you ain't back here by tomorrow night."

"For what — disturbing the peace?" Ledbetter asked dryly.

"Nope — for jailbreaking."

Aaron stiffened as surprise, and then anger struck him. Sam Back was setting him up good. "Maybe we'd better forget the whole thing," he said quietly.

The lawman was unperturbed. "Oh, don't figure there's much chance of that happening. Man just doesn't go back on his promise."

Ledbetter leaned against the wall. "How about a promise from you?"

"I'm making it. Minute you turn that girl over to me you're free to ride on."

Aaron, satisfied as much as he could be, said, "Guess that's it. How do I reach this place — Devil's Creek — where Vedic's holed up?"

The lawman glanced to the window. "Not so fast! You just can't go walking out that door in broad daylight. Folks think you're my prisoner."

Ledbetter grinned tightly as his respect for the conniving old marshal raised another notch. "Means I've got to make a real jailbreak, that it?"

"More or less. Leastwise, got to make it look real. Best we wait until dark."

Sam Back had it all figured out, down to the last buttonhole. And like it or not, he'd have to go along. Aaron smiled faintly. If this ever got out it would furnish a lot of laughs for the boys in the saloons; he, Aaron Ledbetter, helping the law!

"Something funny?"

The gunman shook his head. "Nothing special. How about this Devil's Creek; ever been there?"

Back made himself comfortable on the corner of his desk. "Good many times when the camp was working. Few years ago the ore ran out, town just naturally died."

"Didn't know it was a town."

"Sure. Stores and everything."

"Anybody else living there now?"

"Don't think so. Was one old prospector. Figured there was some silver left and was trying to find it. Expect he drifted on, or maybe died."

"Any idea how Vedic's got things set up?"

"Most likely him and his bunch are living in the old hotel. Only stone building around — rest was nothing but board-and-tar-paper shacks."

"What's it like inside?"

"Same as any other hotel, near as I can recollect. Lobby and a saloon. Dozen or so rooms on the second floor." Sam glanced at the window. "Getting close to suppertime. How about you stepping back into that cell — just in case somebody drops by — while I go rustle you a plate of vittles."

Ledbetter pulled himself away from the wall, reentered the iron cage. The lawman closed the door softly, locked it.

"Back directly," he said, and turning, crossed the room and moved out into the gathering dusk.

Alone, Aaron Ledbetter stared unseeing at the bars. If his situation wasn't so serious it would be a huge joke — this being jockeyed into a bind where he was forced to help an old has-been lawman do his job.

But it was far from a laughing matter. Pete Vedic was a dangerous man, a killer when things were right and necessity presented itself. And

53

the same went for the men who made up his gang. He'd seen them in action once, and they never held back for anything.

Kidnapping. . . . He wondered when Pete Vedic had switched to that brand of outlawry. Pete was more the bank-robbing, stagecoach-holdup kind. Aaron was a little surprised that the outlaw would dabble in kidnapping; it would hardly be profitable in an area where there weren't many persons valuable enough to grab and hold for ransom. He'd certainly made a bust kidnapping the daughter of a small-time rancher and expecting to collect five thousand dollars on her; like as not the rancher hadn't seen that much money in his entire life.

A time later the door opened and Sam Back reappeared carrying a tray. Opening the cell, he placed a meal of steak, potatoes, and coffee before Ledbetter.

"Took a mite longer'n I figured, but I was getting things set for you," he said.

Aaron, suddenly hungry, began to eat.

"Just got word," the marshal said. "Ev Feak raised the money. Borrowed from his brother."

Ledbetter paused. "Good. He pays off and they turn the girl loose. No need for me —"

"Don't change nothing," the lawman said bluntly. "Thing you got to do now is get her and the money back. . . . Both."

Temper and exasperation rocked Ledbetter. "Just what the hell you think —"

"Be no problem for you," Sam Back said

mildly. "I put your horse in the stable. Figured it'd look better."

Aaron relaxed wearily. "What'll I be riding?"

"My black. Tied up out in back."

Aaron stared at the old man. "So it'll be horse stealing on top of jailbreak."

"Well, if you want to look at it that way. Only, I've got your word —"

"All right," Ledbetter said resignedly. "This Devil's Creek, how do I get there?"

"Head north out of town. When you come to a fork in the road, take the left. Goes straight to the camp."

Finished with his food, Aaron rose. Sam Back took the tray, placed it on his desk. Opening a drawer, he produced Ledbetter's pistol, handed it to him.

"Expect you'd better be on your way."

Ledbetter examined the weapon, dropped it into its holster. Crossing to the window, he glanced up and down the street. Except for two men on the porch of a saloon, it was deserted.

The lawman said: "Remember now, got to make this look good."

"You're right, Marshal," Aaron said with a dry grin, and whirling swiftly, he drew his gun and dubbed the lawman over the head.

The blow thudded solidly. Sam Back, a slightly surprised look on his face, crumpled to the floor.

Immediately Ledbetter stepped to the door and opened it a narrow distance. The street, filling with deep shadows, was still empty. Stepping out, he crossed the front of the jail, turned down the side. The lawman's horse was a dozen paces away.

Mounting, he swung about. The north end of town, Sam had said. That meant he had to travel almost the full length of the settlement. He'd be taking plenty of risk, but there was no other choice. Swinging to his right, he located a narrow alleyway and proceeded along its littered course. At least he was keeping off the street.

He rode on, grateful for the closing darkness. Noise was coming from the Castlerock and one of the other saloons, but most of Chacosa's residents were home at that hour, having their evening meal. Later they'd be out strolling the sidewalks, soaking in some of the evening coolness.

Two men were standing at the rear of a building to his right. Watching them narrowly, he pulled the black to a slow walk. They were engaged in a discussion of some sort, and neither paid him any attention as he passed. Aaron shrugged, dispelling the tension that gripped him, continued the quiet march. Looking ahead, he saw the end of the row of structures. The road should lie beyond the last.

Ledbetter pulled up short. A squat man, one he vaguely recalled seeing in the Castlerock, stood before him, blocking his passage. A rifle was in the man's hands.

"Hold up — right there! Seen you coming so I'm all set. You want to keep living, don't reach for that gun of yours. . . . What'd you do, knock old Sam over the head and steal his horse?"

Aaron groaned quietly. "Could be," he replied after a moment. "No sense in you getting hurt. Stand aside."

"You ain't hurting nobody — not while I got this rifle pointed at you," the man said, and then shouted: "Hey, somebody! Help! Help!"

Ledbetter drove his spurs deep into the black's flanks, veered sharply to one side. The rifle exploded and Aaron drew fast, snapped a bullet into the dust at the man's feet. The fellow yelled, dropped his weapon, and leaped back.

Aaron's horse, panicked by the sudden noise and violence, reared and plunged forward, bearing straight down on the man. Ledbetter, leaning wide, lashed out with his fist. He caught the fellow a glancing blow on the side of the head. It did no harm, simply rocked him off-balance, sent him sprawling, as the black rushed by.

A few moments later Ledbetter was on the road to Devil's Creek, with his horse moving at top speed. Glancing over his shoulder, he grinned wryly into the darkness; that should make the jailbreak look real enough for Marshal Sam Back.

7

The moon was up, and Ledbetter had no difficulty following the road. He should reach
Devil's Creek in good time, he estimated, and
began to wonder how he could explain to Pete
Vedic his unexpected appearance.

He could hardly term it accidental; the outlaw's camp was far off the main trails and no
traveler would stray so widely from course. Best
he say it was intentional, he decided finally, and
from that point allow matters to shape themselves.

He glanced around. The long flat he had been
crossing was disappearing, and he was entering a
land of low, round-topped hills studded with
cedar and clumps of rabbit brush. Far beyond,
the irregular rim of higher mountains was etched
against the blue-black of the sky. Devil's Creek
would lie somewhere along the foot of those for-
mations.

At that moment he heard the pound of hooves.
Not entirely certain at first, he drew the black to
a halt and listened. The steady drumming
reached him clearly then, and he frowned. A
posse? All things considered, it seemed hardly
possible — but it could be nothing else.

Urging the black into a lope, he fell to wondering whose idea to pursue it had been. It didn't seem likely Sam Back would carry the farce to that extent unless, to save face, he had been compelled to agree. That probably was the answer. He smiled, wondering what the marshal would do if he simply halted, awaited their arrival. His smile broadened; the cagey old lawman would think of something, he could be sure of that.

The sound of the approaching horses grew louder. Ledbetter began to look around for a place where he might find good cover. A quarter mile farther on, the road began to curve southward, slice a path through a dense stand of scrubby trees and gray-headed sagebrush. Immediately he swung into a thicket and halted.

The posse was not long in arriving — Sam Back and three riders. Ledbetter watched them sweep into view around the bend, gradually slow. The marshal, in the lead, lifted his hand, and they all came to a halt. Sam turned then, began to speak.

The distance was too great for Aaron to hear what was being said, but apparently it was a question whether, with only four men, they should continue, since it was apparent the fugitive was heading straight for the outlaw stronghold at Devil's Creek.

The vote was in the negative, for after a few minutes the posse wheeled about and began to retrace its way along the road. Sam Back had evidently convinced them he'd find another way to apprehend his jailbreaking-horse stealing prisoner. The old lawman, secure in his knowledge of the future, would lay it on thick; his promises would be strong and deep-seated, and since the likelihood of their coming to pass was better than good, the benefit he'd reap was large.

Ledbetter stalled a quarter hour until he was certain the posse was well on its way to Chacosa, and then resumed the trail. Almost at once he saw why Back and the three riders had halted at the bend; ahead, a short distance up the long slope of the mountain, several lights winked in the darkness. He was nearer Devil's Creek than he had imagined.

Allowing the black to choose an easy gait, he rode on. Vedic would have men on guard somewhere along the approach, and it was best he make his arrival openly.

Watching the squares of light grow steadily, he kept to the center of the road, aware that he was moving into the mouth of a wide canyon. He crossed a small stream, which he guessed to be the source of the camp's name, and began a somewhat steep climb. The scrub growth gave way to larger timber, and here and there huge rocks overhung the trail.

Ledbetter would have felt more comfortable elsewhere — or at least with a pistol in his hand. To ride blindly into hostile country knowing he could only accept whatever came at him without opposition was not his customary way of doing things. *Damn Sam Back anyway,* he muttered silently.

"Far enough, mister!"

The command came as no surprise. He brought the black to a halt, looking toward a bulge of rock from behind which the voice had come.

"Get your hands up."

Aaron raised his arms slowly. From the tail of his eye he saw the speaker move in from one side, pistol leveled. Sound on the opposite shoulder of the trail told him a second man was there. He felt a lessening of weight against his thigh as his weapon was removed from its holster.

"Where you think you're going?" the outlaw to his left demanded, stepping back.

Ledbetter looked down at him. He was a stranger, not one of the regulars. "Up to Pete Vedic's camp."

The man's head came up. "Pete know you?"

"Take me to him and find out."

"Little bit on the smart side, ain't you, friend?" the outlaw said, his voice lifting. "We got a way of handling nosey saddle tramps —"

"Maybe we better do what he says, Jess," the second man cut in. "Could be Pete's expecting him."

"Didn't say nothing to me about it."

"Might've forgot — and anyway he ain't in the habit of telling us what's on his mind."

Jess considered briefly, nodded. He motioned to Aaron. "Hang both your hands on that saddle

61

horn — and keep them there. You hear? Get the horses, Turk."

The second outlaw, still not visible to Ledbetter, moved off into the brush, returned a moment later. The pair mounted, and with Jess leading the way, continued on up the trail.

Shortly the canyon flared into a wide basin, and the lights Aaron had seen earlier became clearly defined windows in a two-storied rock building nestled into the south slope of the bowl.

Ledbetter looked around. There was little substantial remaining of the mining camp. Crowding in from both sides of what had once been a street were numerous shacks and huts, all in the last stages of decay. A few signs still hung from rotting posts; only one, erected on a pipe near the center of the settlement, was yet legible. LINCOLN STREET, it proclaimed, obviously commemorating the country's onetime president.

Jess swung toward the hotel. At that a third outlaw emerged from the long shadows beyond the stone building and advanced slowly.

"That you, Jess?"

"Yep, me and Turk. Got us a visitor."

"Visitor? You know what Vedic said about letting drifters come poking up the canyon. Who —"

"Ain't asked his name. Claims he knows Pete."

The newcomer stepped in close, eyes raking Aaron. His jaw dropped. "Jesus!" he muttered.

"The Widowmaker!"

Jess, swinging from the saddle, caught himself, hung there for a moment, and then gradually completed the dismount. Turk swore feelingly.

Jess, on solid ground, turned, stared at Ledbetter. "Reckon you know how things is. We got orders from Pete, and, well, I ain't never seen you before."

Ledbetter said, "Forget it. How about taking me to Pete?"

"Sure — right away."

Aaron came off the black, settled his eyes on Jess. "Don't run off with that," he said, pointing to his pistol in the outlaw's waistband.

Jess nodded and started up the steps for the hotel's door. The man who had come from the shadows spoke.

"Reckon I ought to put his horse away?"

Jess turned impatiently. "Now, how the hell would I know —"

"Put him away," Ledbetter broke in. "Expect I'll be around for a spell."

8

Tense, uncertain as to what his reception by the outlaw chief would be, Aaron followed Jess into the cool, shadowy interior of the building. It was easy to see why no posse dared attack the camp; the hotel, with its two-foot-thick rock walls, was a veritable fortress.

But it was showing the ravages of time and neglect. The lobby was littered with trash blown in by passing winds and discarded by men for want of a better place to throw it. What furniture remained was in shambles, and the faded lithographs and stuffed deer heads on the walls were ragged, ripped by bullets and hanging in shreds.

They crossed the lobby, passed through an archway over which the tattered remnants of once-elegant green and gold portieres still hung, and stepped down into a large adjoining room. A splintered bar sagged against one wall, and Ledbetter guessed this was the saloon Sam Back had mentioned.

Vedic's men had collected all the hotel's usable furniture and assembled it here, converting the area into a sort of general quarters where apparently everything but cooking and sleeping was conducted. There were six men and five women visible. Counting Jess, Turk, and the one who looked after the horses, Vedic's gang tallied nine riders — and there could be others elsewhere on the premises. . . . Vedic's following had increased somewhat.

"Pete," Jess called, halting just inside the arch. "Caught this — this man coming up the trail. Says he's a friend of yourn."

At a table in a far corner of the room, the outlaw leader turned about in his chair. He was engaged in a card game with a woman and two of his gang. Aaron felt surprise run through him. Pete Vedic had aged considerably. His bushy yellow hair was streaked with gray; his face sagged; and his odd round eyes looked faded and watery.

"Bring him over here."

In the hush that dropped over the room, the others paused to watch. Jess jerked his head at Ledbetter, and together they moved through the thin scatter of tables.

"Pogue says he's the one they call the Widowmaker," the outlaw said as they came to a halt at the table.

Pete Vedic's mouth dropped into a crooked smile. "Pogue's right. You ain't got much sense."

Jess swore roughly. "How the hell was I supposed to know who he was? You just told me to watch —"

"All right — all right!" Vedic said, raising his hands in protest. "You done fine — I'm just a mite surprised that you're still alive."

65

The young outlaw shrugged, handed over Ledbetter's pistol. "Here's his iron. . . . Reckon I'd better be getting back. . . . Me and Turk. . . ."

Vedic reached out his hand, took the weapon from Jess, who wheeled and stomped from the room, and examined it absently. He paid particular attention to the inset gold pieces. Finally he raised his eyes lazily.

"Been a long time since Medicine Bow."

"Long time," Aaron agreed.

"Mind telling me what you're doing here?"

There was a faint edge to the outlaw's voice. Ledbetter glanced around the room at the expectant faces. There was no mistaking the sullen hostility.

"Looking for you."

Pete Vedic's eyes flickered with surprise. "Me? Why?"

"Heard you and your boys were holed up here. Thought maybe I might find a game worth sitting in."

Vedic continued to stare in that wide, unblinking way of his. He laid the pistol on the table. "How'd you know I was here?"

Ledbetter forced a short laugh. "You think it's a secret? Everybody knows you're here."

Vedic's mouth drew into a hard, colorless line. He swore vividly. "Knew I shouldn't have let them boys ride into Cimarron! Probably shot off their traps to the whole county."

"Don't think you got much to worry about," Aaron said, shaking his head. "Could hold off

66

the Army in this place." Again he glanced around, wondering where they had the girl; probably locked in one of the upstairs rooms. "How about that game?"

Vedic yawned. "Could be. Boys are sort of resting up, taking things easy. Ain't sure how anxious they'll be to play against you, however."

"If it'll make them feel any better, my luck's been running downhill. Has been for a couple of months. Doubt if I'll hurt anybody's pocketbook much."

Vedic smiled indolently, addressed the room in general. "Any you jaspers feel like setting in with a real expert?"

Aaron felt the pressure within him ease slightly. Vedic had believed him. . . . Now — if he could locate the girl. . . .

The two men at Vedic's table wagged their heads. "Not tonight," one said. "Heard of him. Aim to be full wide awake when I start risking my money."

Pete shifted his gaze to the bar, where several men and two women were standing. "Anybody?"

As one they, too, declined. "Come morning," said a tall, older individual Aaron remembered from Medicine Bow as being called Kansas, "I'll be willing."

Vedic brought his attention back to Ledbetter. "Seems the boys sort of want to rest up before they take you on."

"You?"

"I'll pass. Tomorrow'll be better. Where you aiming to sleep tonight?"

"Be obliged if you'd put me up."

"No sweat. One thing we've got in this dump is plenty of rooms."

"And women," Aaron said, hoping to learn something of Melanie Feak.

Vedic's brows lifted. "Hell! Didn't think they ever bothered you none." He settled back, winked broadly at the overblown, brassy blonde sitting across the table from him. "Always carry ours with us — them and plenty of whiskey. Keeps the boys from getting restless and wanting to go to town." He waved at a chair. "Set down. We'll have a couple of drinks."

Ledbetter started to comply. As he did so the two men rose and moved off. He took one of the vacated seats, smiling at the blonde, who regarded him with thoughtful interest. Vedic wiped out a glass with his forefinger, filled it from the bottle, and shoved it at Aaron.

"This here's Florinda," he said, nodding at the girl. "Sort of my private property — leastwise for the time being."

Florinda's lips compressed into a tight line and her eyes snapped. Vedic reached out, pinched her on one cheek. She jerked back angrily.

Ledbetter downed the raw liquor. "She the only one taken?"

Pete waved indefinitely at the room. "Couple, three more around. Just sort of belong to the

68

bunch. Don't think anybody'd get riled was you to take a fancy to one."

Aaron studied his empty glass. Dead end. "Don't want to do any trespassing," he said, and switched to a different tack. "Things going all right with you? Seems I remember your luck was hitting bottom at Medicine Bow."

"For a fact," the outlaw said, refilling the glasses. "I ain't forgot that double-eagle you staked me to that night in the Staghorn. Do my paying up right now."

The incident had escaped Ledbetter. He nodded, picked up the coin tossed onto the table, rubbed it between his fingers.

"No need for this. . . ."

"Hell there ain't. Nobody can say Pete Vedic don't pay his debts — especially when things are going good."

"Glad to hear it."

"Be getting my hands on a right smart of cash tomorrow."

Ledbetter feigned surprise. "You riding out?"

"Nope. This time I'm setting on my backside letting it come to me."

"Good way to be working. This cash — it be available for a game?"

"Sure, why not? If the cards ain't running for you might be the right time to take you on. I'd admire owning that fancy gun you're carrying."

"When I'm down to it, I quit."

"How about them gold pieces in the handle?"

"Been dug out a couple of times. Always

manage to get them back before I'm done."

Vedic yawned again. "Always a first time for something."

He frowned, looked toward the archway. Pogue, a pair of saddlebags looped over his arm, was entering the room.

"Look here, Pete," the outlaw said, dropping the pouches on the table. "Know it don't make much sense, but I took them off the horse he was riding."

Sam Back's saddlebags. Aaron watched coolly as Vedic reached into the pockets, began to dig around. The outlaw drew forth a sheaf of folded papers — wanted posters — from one; in the other he found a small notebook and a box of rifle cartridges. Vedic went through the dodgers and the notebook methodically, stuffed them back into the pouches, and cast a sideways glance at Aaron.

"You a lawman nowadays?"

Ledbetter laughed. "Sure. Make a hell of a good living at it."

"Maybe he's turned bounty hunter," Pogue suggested in a serious voice.

Again Aaron laughed. "Could collect me a pile around here, couldn't I? Only that's not it. Horse belongs to the marshal in Chacosa. Had me a bit of trouble there and had to borrow the first one I came to."

Vedic's brows raised. "You stole the marshal's horse — old Sam Back's?"

"Was sort of in a hurry. Never had time to ask

who he belonged to."

The outlaw stared at him for a long moment and then began to laugh. "Sure ties me good — rustling a lawman's horse! Man, you're going to have to learn — leave them kind alone!"

Ledbetter felt the tension lift within the room, felt his own nerves level off. The explanation had been acceptable, thanks to his own reputation.

Vedic picked up the bags, tossed them to Pogue. "Put 'em back. Expect he'll be wanting to return them first chance he gets."

"He can have the dodgers," Aaron said, carrying the joke to its fullest, "but the horse is something else. Got to ride — never was much for walking."

"Get rid of him, too. Ain't much worse thing you can do to a lawman than steal his horse except take his gun away from him. We got some extra broomtails around. I'll have Pogue pick you out one."

"Obliged to you," Aaron said, and then looked to the stairway at the end of the bar that climbed to the upper floor. Two more of Vedic's gang — a man and a girl. They started down the dust-covered steps.

Ledbetter felt the quick build of pressure once again. The man was Les Brunkman, a quarrelsome troublemaker forever on the prod. He'd had a run-in with him up in Miles City a few months previous. It would have resulted in a shoot-out if he hadn't chosen to ignore the man.

But the situation was different now. Eyes narrowing, he watched the couple reach the bottom of the stairs, saw Brunkman glance his way and pull up short.

9

In that next moment Aaron Ledbetter realized that where Les Brunkman was concerned the situation had not changed at all. But he could afford no altercation with the man, regardless of the smoldering ill will their previous meeting had fashioned. It would have to wait until after he had located Melanie Feak, returned her to Chacosa, and cleared himself with Marshal Sam Back.

Ignoring Brunkman, he shifted his attention to the girl. She was young, pretty, and clad in a garish red and yellow dress that failed completely in its efforts to fit her slender figure. She was paying no mind to Brunkman, was instead smiling at Pete Vedic. Ledbetter glanced at Florinda. The blonde was glaring at the girl, her lips tight, an aggressive set to her chin. That there was trouble between them was apparent.

"Well — if it ain't the big man!"

At the sound of the sarcastic words, Aaron shifted his gaze back to Brunkman, who had moved up to the outlaw chief's table. The girl had pulled away from him slightly and was standing beside Vedic's chair.

"Figured I'd maybe someday run into you again," Brunkman said in a voice that carried throughout the room.

Pete Vedic looked up. "You know Ledbetter?"

Brunkman, his wide flat face broken by an unpleasant grin, nodded, drew up a chair. "Sure I know him. . . . We're old friends."

Ledbetter, arms resting on the table, studied the backs of his hands, fought off the temper pushing through him.

"Had us a little run-in up Montana way," Lee continued, reaching for the whiskey. "That's how good friends we are."

Vedic was immediately interested. "Yeh?"

"Your big man here turned tail — walked out just as things was getting interesting."

Ledbetter's head came up slowly. "Drop it, Brunkman," he said in a flat, emotionless tone.

Pete Vedic came completely about on his chair to look at his second in command. "You mean you tried to rag him into — why, you damned fool! You plain damned fool!"

Les lowered his glass. Color seeped into his face. "Now, wait a minute, Pete. I don't take —"

"You better take it!" Vedic snapped. "He'll kill you so quick you'll never know what happened."

Brunkman grunted. "You been listening to a lot of windy talk, Pete."

"Don't have to listen," the outlaw replied. "I know." He turned to Aaron. "You ain't saying much about this."

Ledbetter shrugged. "Nothing to say. Had a reason for what I did in Miles City. Brunkman got the wrong idea."

"Anytime you want to take up where we left off —" Les said, bristling.

"Settle down," Vedic cut in. "Best thing you can do is forget it."

"Ain't forgetting nothing."

"Leave him be," Florinda said, coming into the conversation. "Let him get his head blowed off. Be a big help to everybody."

Brunkman swung to the blonde, mouth working angrily. "You'll never see the day!" he snarled.

She gave him a wooden smile. "I can keep hoping."

Pete Vedic swore in disgust, shook his head at Aaron. "Nice friendly folks I got around me. . . . All hate each other's guts." He turned his watery eyes to Les. "Go on outside — cool off."

"What for? I ain't backing down to this four-flusher."

"Then you better be picking out your tombstone. I've seen you both working. You ain't got a Chinaman's chance."

"We'll see about that," Brunkman shot back, thoroughly aroused. "I'm ready anytime — anywhere."

Vedic sighed, lifted his hands, let them fall in a gesture of helplessness. "All right, all right. Ain't no getting through that bull head of yours. But hold off till after tomorrow — understand?"

Brunkman poured himself another drink. "Up to him," he said, looking at Aaron.

To Ledbetter, Vedic said: "That suit you?"

Aaron moved his shoulders slightly. Evidently Les had something to do with the ransom; likely he was the one designated to pick up the money from Feak.

"Whatever you say, Pete."

"It ain't Pete that's got the say!" Brunkman yelled, and pushed back his chair. "We'll settle this —"

Vedic was up instantly, blocking the man. "Keep your shirt on, goddamn it! If I wasn't needing you, I'd let you go ahead, get yourself filled full of holes. Now, go on, like I told you!"

Brunkman hesitated, glared past the outlaw chief's shoulder at Aaron. "This ain't over, mister!"

Ledbetter casually reached for his glass. "No, I expect not," he murmured disinterestedly.

Pete resumed his chair. Les wheeled, swaggered toward the bar and the man standing there, obviously feeling that he'd won a victory and proven himself. Sooner or later they'd come to grips, Aaron knew. He stirred restlessly. There was no end to it; there never would be until he himself lay dead.

"Ain't she something?"

Pete Vedic's gloating voice roused him from his dark thoughts. He looked up. "What?"

"This here new gal of mine — ain't she something?" the outlaw repeated, drawing the girl closer.

Ledbetter nodded to her, and she smiled back. "Brunkman's?"

"Hell, no!" Vedic said. "Les's trying powerful hard, but I'm keeping her for myself." He glanced at Florinda a sly grin on his face.

The blonde's lips curled scornfully. "Nothing but a green kid. Not enough woman for you."

"And you are, eh?"

"More'n enough."

"Maybe I like 'em young — so's I can learn them a thing or two. Now you — can't learn you nothing."

Florinda's eyes dropped. Vedic laughed. "And she's got money — cash money. Can't hardly beat that hand — young, pretty as a moonflower, and money."

Ledbetter looked at the girl. She was leaning against the outlaw, obviously enjoying the moment. Florinda raised her gaze to the girl. The same hatred for Brunkman that Aaron had noted earlier glowed now for the girl.

"Keep away from him," the older woman said in a low voice. "I'm warning you. He ain't got sense enough to leave you alone, but I can damn sure keep —"

"I'll do what I please," the girl interrupted lightly. "If Mr. Vedic wants —"

"Mr. Vedic!" Florinda mimicked. She turned, looked out into the room. "You all hear that — *Mr. Vedic!*"

The outlaw's eyes narrowed. He lashed out quickly, backhanded the blonde across the mouth. The saloon was abruptly silent as Florinda settled into her chair, putting her fingers to her bruised lips.

Les Brunkman pushed away from the bar, recrossed to the table. "What's going on?"

Vedic shook his head. "Nothing."

Les glanced at Florinda and laughed, then brought his attention to the girl. "Thought maybe me and you could take us a little walk."

"She ain't going nowhere," Vedic said before the girl could reply.

Brunkman's color rose again. "Reckon I got something to say —"

"You ain't got nothing to say!" the outlaw chief roared. "Get that in your goddamn head, Les! Seems to me you're getting mighty big for your britches lately. First thing you know you'll be forgetting who's running this outfit — and that sure won't be healthy."

Abruptly he got to his feet, faced the others in the room. "Something else I'm going to say. Don't want none of you — nobody — messing around with this here little gal. It's hands off — you got that straight? I'm taking her for mine."

The silence continued. Brunkman stared at Pete Vedic for a long minute and then suddenly wheeled and struck for the archway, followed by a thin, misshapen man who had been next to him at the bar.

Vedic remained rigid, glaring at those who yet remained, and then finally sat down. His mood switched immediately as a smile pulled at his lips. He took the girl's hand, squeezed it, and nodded at Aaron.

"Reckon you ain't met this old friend of mine. Name's Ledbetter — only that ain't what folks usually call him."

The girl inclined her head. "I'm pleased to know you," she said politely. "You can call me Melly."

10

Aaron Ledbetter's expression did not change as surprise flooded through him. Melly — short for Melanie. It could be coincidence . . . yet — He started to ask, abandoned the thought. It might arouse suspicion on the part of Pete Vedic.

Nodding pleasantly, he took up his glass, toasted the girl with the liquor still remaining. "Luck. . . . From what I gather, you're new around here."

Melly flashed a quick look at Florinda, bobbed her head. Pete Vedic slid his arms about her, drew her close.

"Brand, spanking new," he said possessively.

She could be no one else but Melanie Feak. Aaron studied her through hooded eyes, struggling to reconcile the girl Sam Back had spoken of with the one he was seeing now. A rancher's daughter — simple, young, innocent.

Melly appeared to be far from that, but she could be playing a part, he realized suddenly. She could be playing a desperate game designed to gain time while she sought frantically for a means to escape the outlaws. He wished there was some way he could get word to her, let her know he was there to help, but with Vedic close by he judged it best to take no chance.

The outlaw chief said: "Obliged to you for pulling in your horns with Les. He don't mean nothing to me excepting I got a little job for him in the morning. After that he's your meat, if you're wanting."

"Up to him," Ledbetter answered. "Got no quarrel far as I'm concerned."

Vedic stirred lazily, released Melly, and reached for the bottle. "Well, he sure has with you — or thinks he has. Was I you, I'd keep my eyes peeled."

Taking up his glass, he filled it with whiskey and handed it to the girl. She forced a smile, accepting the drink hesitantly.

"Go ahead," Vedic said.

"I — I've never drunk much —"

"Time you was learning. Do you good."

Melly raised the glass to her lips, took a swallow of the fiery liquor. She gagged, coughed as tears flooded into her eyes. The outlaw laughed.

"See there? Bet you liked it."

Melly placed the glass on the table, wiped at her eyes. "Maybe I'd better start slow —"

"Better not start at all," Florinda said flatly, and turned to Ledbetter. "Where you headed for, Mister Widowmaker?"

Aaron smothered the irritation the name always provoked, said, "El Paso — Juárez City."

"Want some company?"

Ledbetter hesitated. "Hard trip."

"She ain't going nowhere," Vedic said, apparently listening for all his preoccupation with Melly. "Nobody walks out on Pete Vedic — man or woman — unless I say so."

Florinda shrugged. "If you think I'm hanging around here while you —"

"You are if I say so!" Vedic snapped.

Ledbetter's glance was on Melly. Her eyes were sparkling, and it was evident she enjoyed the discord she had aroused. But she was overplaying her hand; Florinda was dangerous and not one to be trifled with.

Vedic, beginning to show the effects of the whiskey he had consumed, leaned toward the blonde. "Ain't no reason why you two can't get along. Hell — I'm man enough for both of you!"

Melly's face clouded. She looked down at him. "I thought you said we —" she began, and then checked her words.

Pete grinned at her. "You mean that there deal we got going? Sure I said it — and I mean it."

Florinda laughed, a harsh, grating sound. "He'll promise you anything, kid, to get what he wants. Ask me, I know."

The outlaw's face darkened as his mouth pulled into a crooked smile. He pointed his finger at the blonde. "Why don't you just trot off to bed? Maybe a night's sleep'll do you some good."

"Just what I aim to do," the older woman snapped, and got to her feet. She started around the table, paused beside Melly. "You better be doing the same — and if you've got any brains you'll lock your door."

Vedic threw back his head and laughed. Florinda glared at him briefly, and stiff with anger, marched to the stairway and began to ascend.

Melly watched her for a moment. Then, disengaging herself from the outlaw's grasp, she said, "I think I'll go, too. I'm a little tired."

"Sure, sure," Pete said genially. " 'Bout time we was all turning in." He drained his glass, added, "Don't pay Florinda no mind."

"I won't," the girl replied. "Good night."

Vedic's brows lifted, dropped back into a bunched line. "Good night," he mumbled.

Others in the room were moving toward the archway, some veering to climb the steps, the rest cutting off into the lobby, pointing for the street beyond, where they would have a final smoke and a look at the night.

Pete Vedic rose. "You'll be needing a bed. Room off the lobby — behind the desk. Come on, I'll show you."

Ledbetter, maintaining close surveillance over Melly, said, "No need."

The outlaw shrugged. "Suit yourself," he replied, and headed for the street also.

Aaron, continuing to delay, poured himself a short drink, sat with it raised to his lips. He watched the girl gain the upper landing, casually turn down the hall, switching her hips in a leisurely, provocative way.

Waiting until he saw which door she entered, and marking it in his mind, he finished off the whiskey, rose, and went in search of the quarters assigned him. He paused beside the battered desk to glance at the doorway and the long shadows in Lincoln Street outside. He hoped Pete Vedic and his men would turn in soon; there wasn't much time left before daylight.

11

Melly, flushed by Pete Vedic's attention and inwardly glowing at the jealousy she had aroused in Florinda, opened the door to her room and stepped inside. She closed the panel softly, stood for a time considering the key in the lock, and then turned away, leaving it untouched.

Crossing to the bed, she sat down, irritated as always by the dry squeak of springs, which reminded her of home, and began to unlace her spool-heeled high shoes. She paused, her thoughts for some reason moving to the stranger she had met downstairs — Ledbetter.

There was something attractive yet repelling about the man. He was handsome in a rough-hewn sort of way, but his eyes — so flat and withdrawn — chilled her, while at the same time they held her with a strange fascination.

He was not like the other men in Pete Vedic's gang, who gave her bold stares and made whispered suggestions and were forever trying to get her alone. She guessed that would stop now. Pete had made it plenty clear how things stood where she was concerned.

Les certainly hadn't liked that. Since she'd arrived he'd sort of taken over, seemed to assume she was his woman. He was wasting his time. She was after larger game — Pete Vedic himself, and it looked as if she had him; he'd as much as said so, and as soon as her pa paid the ransom there'd be no doubt.

Les Brunkman had some ideas about Vedic, too. He'd let it slip earlier that evening that he thought Pete was about finished, that the time was ripe for him to take over the gang. Pete was getting old, he'd said, and the bunch was going to split wide open and drift away unless somebody with guts and new ideas grabbed the reins.

Les had even hinted that it might be necessary to get rid of Pete for good when the time came, and mentioned that people'd be smart to side with him. But she'd played it cozy and avoided making any commitments one way or another. Personally, Melly wasn't so sure Brunkman was man enough to take over; Pete Vedic had certainly made him toe the mark when he shot off his mouth in front of Ledbetter. Could be Les was underestimating Pete. Regardless, she'd not tip one way or the other until she knew exactly who'd be ruling the roost.

It pleased her, sent little chills running up her spine, to realize she was not only a part but the center of this world of violent men and what her pa would term deadly sin. Reared in a frugal home where the observance of the rantings of a fire-and-brimstone preacher was the way of life, she found her new situation a complete reversal of all she had ever been taught, a soaring rebellion against all she had ever known.

She gloried in it, and while the thought that she could be playing a dangerous game never entered her mind, such realization would have made little difference. She was free. She had thrown off the bonds of parental restraint that made of her a nobody and was now a person of importance.

That was what counted most — being someone of importance, being the object of every man's glance — something that had come to pass only after she'd discarded the high-necked, floor-length Mother Hubbard she had been compelled to wear and clothed herself in a gaudy, sequined dress that was neither long nor high. And Florinda, who fancied herself quite a woman and who had been Vedic's favorite for a long time apparently, was beginning to fear for her place in the scheme of things.

Imagine that! She — mousy little Melly Feak who'd never been permitted to so much as look at a boy much less be alone with one — about to displace the favored and become queen to the king of the outlaws! It was unbelievable, and just as exciting as the story in that yellow-paged book she'd found one day along the roadside.

She rose and crossed to the washstand, over which hung a portion of a mirror. Holding the lamp just so, she examined her face. She was pretty, she guessed, now that she'd been able to fix her hair differently, and with the aid of rouge and rice powder borrowed from one of the girls, erase some of that healthy farmerish look she so despised. And she was young. That's what seemed to count most with Pete Vedic — and that's where she had it all over Florinda, who must be at least thirty.

She hoped she could avoid getting that hard, worn look that marred the faces of Florinda and the others. Liquor probably was the cause, and as soon as she had matters arranged with Pete, she'd refrain from drinking. She hated the stuff, anyway; it made her gag and slightly sick, but Pete Vedic seemed to want her to drink and she needed to get along with him — at least for a while.

Pete. . . . Too bad he wasn't more like Les Brunkman or Ledbetter. He wasn't much for looks, actually was homely as well as being short and a little old. Ledbetter was tall. . . . What was it they called him — the Widowmaker? Melly shuddered a little as she turned and again sat on the edge of the bed. He was a gunman — a killer; they were all afraid of him, even Pete Vedic. She could tell by the way they watched him.

What would it be like to be his woman? Exciting, for sure — standing behind him while he gambled for huge piles of money; waiting while he shot it out with some man who'd challenged him, or perhaps had insulted her.

Maybe if things didn't work out with Pete to suit her, she'd . . . Her thoughts came to a halt. She frowned, recalling Florinda and how Vedic had forbidden her to leave when she had asked Ledbetter about accompanying him to El Paso.

If Pete planned for her to be his woman, why would he object to Florinda's leaving?

She was simply going to have to reach a better understanding with Pete Vedic. Buying her way into his gang entitled her to some say-so; and she wasn't going to stand for him having a second woman around, like he'd sort of hinted. It was her or nothing, far as she was concerned. If he wouldn't agree to that then she'd take the money her pa would be handing over for her release and ride on with Ledbetter herself.

He had seemed only vaguely interested in her, but that could change; besides, no gambler would ever turn down a five-thousand-dollar dowry. She smiled at having put it that way — a dowry.

But she'd have to act quickly. Ledbetter evidently planned to ride on the next day after he'd played a few hands of cards. And Vedic wanted it that way. He'd put on a show of making him welcome, but that really wasn't how he felt about it.

Maybe it was because he feared Ledbetter would kill Les Brunkman — and Pete didn't want anything happening to Les until the meeting with her pa was over. She guessed she wanted it that way, too. Les Brunkman was sort of important to both of them — for the time being.

She wished now Vedic hadn't told her pa to pay off no one except Les, but she supposed a definite arrangement such as that was necessary. Someone else, possibly another member of the gang, could slip in ahead of time and pick up the money, leaving Pete and her with nothing. Yes, he was right in handling it that way. Being an old hand at the business, he knew how to protect himself.

The best course to follow, she decided, was to talk with Ledbetter, try and persuade him to hang around for a day or two. She'd have to make up some good reason, but if it worked she would then have a chance to talk things over with Pete Vedic, learn where she stood with him, and if he —

A sound outside the door drew her attention. She had a quick recollection of Florinda's warning concerning the lock and rose hurriedly, a wave of fear washing over her.

And then she took firm control of her nerves. She was glad she'd deliberately ignored the blonde woman's warning; now she could have that talk with Pete Vedic.

12

A man eternally keyed to the ever-present possibility of death, Aaron Ledbetter entered the small room off the lobby in a single step, moved quickly to one side. Closing the door with his heel, he listened into the hot, stale-smelling blackness for any unusual sound.

Only silence greeted him, and he guessed he was alone, that no one awaited him in ambush. Reaching into his pocket for a lucifer, he fired it with a thumbnail and glanced around. A lamp stood in dust-covered solitude on a table placed against the back wall. Crossing, he lifted the smoked chimney, turned up the wick, and applied the flame to its charred tip.

Feeble yellow glow spread through the room. Resetting the chimney, Aaron turned. The place was no more than a large closet, had evidently been the quarters of the room clerk during the hotel's heyday. There was a chair, one leg of which was missing, the table, a narrow bed built bunk-style into the wall. A dirt-clogged carpet covered two-thirds of the floor, and on a crudely erected shelf were several discoloring magazines and newspapers. There was no outside window, the cubicle depending entirely on the door opening into the lobby for ventilation.

It didn't matter. Ledbetter had no intention of spending any time in the room; he must get to Melanie Feak, and do it quickly. Dousing the light, he returned to the door, opened it slightly, and looked into the cobwebby lobby. It was deserted, as was the saloon where earlier Pete Vedic and his crowd had gathered. Some of the men were still up, however. He could hear an occasional cough and a spoken word or two coming from the street.

He had no choice but to wait, be patient. They'd all be turning in shortly. He couldn't afford to rush things, get himself caught prowling about the building or entering Melly's room — especially by Vedic or Les Brunkman. He could afford no gunplay at this point. Still, if he delayed too long, lost the advantage of darkness —

He drew back. Two shadowy figures blocked the entrance to the hotel, paused. One flipped a cigarette back into the street, its coal describing a red arc as it soared through the darkness. Then both came on into the lobby, stamped across the barren wood floor toward the stairway.

Aaron peered at them through the crack. Not Vedic or Brunkman. He leaned back, restlessness nagging him. Again he stiffened. A third man was entering from the porch. Les Brunkman this time; he could tell by the thickset shoulders, the thrown-forward head. Brunkman was followed by the outlaw who had tagged after him when Vedic had sent him into the street to cool off.

"Damn sure see about it tomorrow," Les was saying as they passed. "Just could be I'll settle me a couple of things."

There was both threat and promise in Brunkman's voice, and Ledbetter guessed that he himself was involved in the outlaw's plans. Well, Les Brunkman would have to wait for another time, another day; with luck Aaron hoped to be well on his way to Chacosa with the girl by sunup.

He listened to the beat of the man's footsteps, heard them fade and then cease altogether. Vedic . . . where the hell was Pete Vedic? Ledbetter waited out fifteen more minutes, decided he could delay no longer. Time was slipping by at an alarming rate — and he ought to get the fool girl out of her room anyway if, as Florinda had inferred, she had some idea of leaving her door unlocked for Vedic.

Moving quietly, he stepped into the lobby. He crossed to the outside doorway, checked the porch and the street. No one was in sight. Wheeling, he doubled back to the stairway, and treading carefully to avoid loose boards, climbed to the second floor. Streaks of light were showing beneath two of the several doors — one of them Melly's. He halted, gave that consideration.

Pete Vedic could already be with her — or it could be one of the girls, a roommate. Either way it posed a problem, one he could handle quickly if it proved to be a woman. Vedic, however — he shook his head, dismissed it from his mind. He'd skin that snake if and when it presented itself.

He moved off down the hall, hoping for his sake Melly had left the door unlocked, condemning her if she had. Reaching the panel, he paused, listened. There was only silence. Placing his hand on the china knob, he turned it gently. The door gave. He stepped inside quickly.

Melly stood near the bed, eyes wide, lips parted. "You! I didn't —"

"You little fool!" he snarled, unreasonably angry. "Leaving that door unlocked — you're lucky it's me and not Vedic or one of the others."

She stiffened as indignation drove away the shock and surprise at his appearance. "I was hoping it would be Pete Vedic."

"Don't doubt it," he muttered, and turned the key in the lock. It failed to respond. He tried again, swore deeply. The lock was broken. He glanced to her. "Pete put you in this room?"

Melly nodded. He shook his head and crossed to the window, pulled the shade aside and looked out. She watched him, and then, reminding herself not to appear too outraged since she had plans for him should those with Vedic fall through, she spoke.

"What do you want?"

He faced her squarely. "You're Melanie Feak?"

"Yes — why?"

"Came after you."

"Came after me?" she echoed, startled. "Why? Who sent you?"

"Trapped into it by the marshal at Chacosa." He studied her thoughtfully. "This whole deal's rigged, isn't it? Never was a kidnapping. You handed yourself over to Pete Vedic, cooked up the ransom with him."

She ignored his words, asked anxiously: "Did Pa raise the money?"

"Got it from his brother, so the marshal said."

"I figured Uncle Carter would help," she said in a relieved voice.

His jaw hardened. "You any idea what you've put your folks through?"

"They'll get over it," she replied airily, and then added in a more serious vein, "Doubt if it really matters much, anyway."

"It does," he said flatly. "Get your things together. Only chance we have of getting out of this place is while they're all asleep."

Melly drew back a step, frowned. "What do you mean? I'm not leaving."

"Hell you're not!" Ledbetter snapped in a sudden flare of exasperation. "I don't aim to spend the rest of my days dodging lawmen!"

She shook her head stubbornly. "I don't know why you're mixed up in this, and what's more, I don't care. But I'm not going home."

His voice was flat, emotionless. "Get your things. We're leaving."

She did not stir. "I don't want to ever go back.

I like it here — like being a part of all this. And when I give half the money to Pete —"

"It's no life for you," Aaron said, changing his approach and endeavoring to reason with her. "These men are outlaws — renegades. The law's just waiting for them to slip up, make a mistake. And a woman doesn't mean a thing to them. Just a bit of gear to use — like a saddle or a horse, and not half as important."

"I'll be more than that. Once Pete and I are married —"

Ledbetter's jaw sagged. "Married! You think he's going to marry you? Not the marrying kind — none of them are."

"But I'll have the money, and he'll do what I say."

Aaron laughed. "You won't have it long, and when it's gone you'll be finished, too. He'll have what he was after and then he'll turn back to Florinda, or one of her kind."

Melanie looked down, bit at her lips. "Still be better than what I had — or was. A nobody in a prison, drying up, growing old before my time, wearing myself away at a life of drudgery."

"You think that won't happen to you while you're being dragged around from pillar to post by Vedic or Brunkman, or some other owlhoot? You don't know what pure drudgery is!"

"I know," she said in a quiet lost voice. "It's getting up at four every morning, winter and summer. It's cleaning and cooking and washing clothes and endless chores until dark, when you

96

fall into bed with every ounce of your strength gone.

"It's never seeing anyone but Pa and Ma — and the one big thing in life is church on Sunday, only I have to sit with the old women because it's a hellfire sin to even look at a man."

Pity for the girl stirred through Aaron Ledbetter, but he kept his tone firm. "I understand all that. It's hard, but you've got to believe this — it's still beats throwing in with Vedic or anybody like him. A good look at Florinda and the other camp followers hanging around here ought to prove that to you."

"But they've had their time. Me — I had nothing at home — less to look forward to."

Ledbetter, brushing at the sweat on his forehead, abruptly reached the end of his patience. "Arguing is getting us nowhere," he snapped. "I'm taking you back to Chacosa, to the marshal. You're my ticket south. Once that's done, you can do as you damn please — turn around and come back if you like. Only thing that interests me is squaring myself with that badge toter."

She shrugged, smiled. "You can't make me go."

"I can — and you can lay odds on it I will."

Melanie regarded him in silence, doubting, yet afraid not to believe. "I could scream — bring someone in here real quick."

"It might bring Vedic, or maybe Brunkman, but not the others. They've heard women yell for help before."

"You'd be in trouble —"

"Probably mean a killing. Vedic or Brunkman, maybe me."

Her face clouded. "I don't see why it's so important that you take me back."

Aaron wiped at his forehead again, glanced uneasily at the door. "Let's just say I've been walking on thin ice for years. Can't afford to do anything that'll crack it."

Once more she was silent, then: "Suppose I said I'd go with you willingly if you'd make a deal with me. Would you listen?"

Aaron shifted irritably. "Meaning what?"

"Why don't we team up? We'll get the money Pa's paying and —"

"Not a chance," Ledbetter said before she could finish. "Last thing I want is a woman hanging around my neck."

"Well, just take me with you, then. There are plenty like Pete Vedic I could join with. Having all that money —"

Ledbetter swore helplessly. "What the devil's the matter with you? This isn't some kid's game you're talking about! These are tough, hard people you're trying to throw in with. Life means nothing to them."

"Does it to you, Widowmaker?"

He glanced at her sharply. "It does — no matter what you may think or have heard. Anyway, it's not me we're talking about."

"You're right — and it's my life. I think I've got the right to live it the way I want." She paused, looked squarely at him. "What's it to be? Do I make a fuss, or will you take me with you? I give you my promise that once we reach El Paso you'll never see me again."

Ledbetter had reached the point where he was agreeable to anything that would get them out of the old hotel and away from the threat of Pete Vedic and his crowd.

"You're one hell of a bargainer," he said, smiling faintly. "We'll talk about it soon as we're in the clear."

"But we can't leave — we'll have to wait for the money."

He had his own ideas concerning the money, one that entailed intercepting Vedic's messenger in the morning after he had met with Everett Feak and collected the ransom. But he said nothing of it.

"You think Pete'll just hand that money over to you when you tell him you've changed your mind? He'll laugh in your face. We'll have to figure another way to get it."

She thought for a moment, said, "All right — but there's something else. I am a good bargainer, like you said. I won't take a step until I have your promise —"

Melanie paused as Ledbetter raised his hand in swift warning. Both turned to the door, watched as the knob moved experimentally.

13

They'd waited too long.

Aaron Ledbetter swore, cursing the day he'd ever heard of Chacosa. The harder he tried to get out of the tight he was in, the deeper he sank — and all because of a goddamn two-bit lawman who was trying to turn the clock back twenty years!

Furious, he motioned at Melanie to twist down the lamp, and as she did he stepped to one side of the door. The knob moved again and the panel swung inward.

A shadowy figure, arm upraised, lunged into the room. Aaron, waiting, closed in quickly. He clamped one hand about the wrist of the intruder's uplifted arm, the other over the mouth — and was suddenly aware of the odor of cheap perfume, of hair pressing against his face. He drew back.

Florinda!

Removing his fingers from her lips, he wrenched the knife from her grasp and shoved her onto the bed. Reaching back, he closed the door and signaled to Melanie. She stood by the lamp, frozen. He joined her and turned up the wick himself.

Facing Florinda, he said, "What's this all

about?" already knowing the answer.

Pure hate glowed in the blonde woman's eyes. She glared at Melanie. "You little bitch — I'll kill you!"

Aaron considered her in the hot stillness. Her breast was heaving and a fine sweat lay upon her upper lip. He could settle the matter quickly by telling her he was taking Melanie with him, but that might prove dangerous. Florinda would immediately relay that bit of information to Pete Vedic, taunt him with it. And the outlaw chief, planning strongly on the ransom money and already claiming Melly for his own, would react instantly. He'd be lucky, Ledbetter thought grimly, if he didn't have to fight his way through the whole gang.

Florinda, beginning to calm, looked at Melanie and then at Aaron. "What're you doing here?"

Ledbetter seized the opening. "Now, what the hell you think I'm here for?"

The blonde woman's eyes flared briefly with surprise, and then she shrugged. "Thought I'd find Pete with her. He been here?"

"No. Probably turned in."

Florinda shook her head. "Not yet. Been waiting for him."

Uneasiness pushed through Aaron. Pete Vedic was still up and around somewhere — and he could have others with him.

"I'm warning you," he heard Florinda say, "quit egging Pete on. He ain't for you."

101

Melanie, recovered from the initial shock of the attack, threw her head back haughtily. "Nobody tells me what I can do —"

Florinda was off the bed in a sudden catlike leap. Ledbetter, equally fast, caught her by one arm, thrust her again onto the bed.

"She's not interested in Pete," he said. "Ought to see that."

"Then what's she hanging around him for?"

"Got an idea she'd like to stay with your bunch. Just trying to get in with the headman."

Florinda was unsatisfied. "More'n that to it. I've watched her shining up to him."

"Plays up to all of them. I aim to put a stop to it."

The blonde woman's brows arched. "You taking her away with you?"

"Thinking about it."

"When?"

"Haven't done that much thinking. Couple of days, I expect."

Melanie's head came up. "There's no reason to wait a —"

His hard look stilled her. Involuntarily he glanced at the door. Every moment they remained in the old hotel brought them nearer to trouble. But he didn't dare rush Florinda, arouse suspicion; he could only let matters take their course, develop naturally — and hope that Vedic or Brunkman didn't put in an appearance.

"You're a fool to come here," Florinda said. "Pete's apt to drop by any minute, and if he found you with her —"

Again Aaron Ledbetter made the most of an opportunity. "I'd be ready," he said, caressing the pistol on his hip. "Pete's a pretty good old boy, however. I'd hate to kill him. You got some idea where we might go?"

Florinda nodded immediately. "Mine shaft up the slope a piece. Little house there. You know how to get out the back way?"

"No. There a door?"

The blonde woman nodded, pulled herself off the bed. "Come on, I'll show you," she said, starting for the door. Halfway to it she halted, faced Melanie. "You got yourself a man now — so leave mine alone. Hear?"

Ledbetter felt the girl stiffen angrily, saw the rise of more haranguing. "I'll see to that," he said hurriedly.

Florinda, pushing at her loosened hair, turned back to the panel, opened it quietly, and looked up and down the hall. She took a half step, again hesitated.

"When you telling Pete?"

"Tomorrow," Aaron said, hanging tight to his patience.

Satisfied, Florinda moved into the corridor. Aaron, face grim, and keeping a firm grip on Melanie's hand, followed.

At the end of the hall they turned into a narrow offset, halted before a door. Grasping the knob and pressing her body against it, Florinda twisted slowly. The panel opened with a muffled squeak.

"Down the steps — turn right," she murmured. "Path takes you up the slope."

Aaron, pushing Melanie ahead with barely restrained urgency, crowded onto the landing.

"Obliged. . . ."

The blonde woman gave him a worn smile. "For nothing. I'll leave the door ajar so's you can get back in."

Ledbetter, still holding to the girl, started down the narrow stairs. Reaching bottom, he paused. The horses were somewhere to their left. He glanced at the landing to assure himself Florinda had gone. Satisfied, he said, "This way," and cut to the left.

14

Florinda turned back into the dark hall, halted when she heard the slow drag of footsteps in the lobby below. Moving through the shadows, she crossed to the railing at the head of the stairs, and well concealed, looked down.

Vedic, holding himself rigid, came through the archway. Pausing long enough to grab a bottle off the bar, he made his way to a table and settled in a chair. Pete was steadily drinking himself into a state, she realized. He'd be a mean one to be around tomorrow — especially when he found out about Melly and Ledbetter.

Maybe it would be smarter to tell him about that tonight. He'd be coming up to Melly's room shortly; why not be waiting there and hit him square in the face with it when he walked in? He'd raise all hell and take it out on her, but that was nothing new — and she was entitled to a moment of triumph now and then, wasn't she?

She decided it was a good idea, and wheeling, made her way to the girl's quarters. Closing the door, she sat down on the bed to wait. It was not an uncommon occurrence to her — Pete's yielding to the blandishments of another woman — and more than once she'd been asked why she put up with it. What those who questioned her patience didn't know was that she and Pete Vedic were man and wife — legally.

No one was aware of the fact — not even Pete himself. She had caught him at just such a stage of advanced drunkenness, while he was yet mobile but mentally paralyzed, and paid a Laramie parson handsomely to perform the ceremony. Later she had been afraid to tell him, and thus it had rocked on — with her his woman in both truth and fancy.

She guessed she really did love Pete, regardless of his multitudinous faults, and she supposed that he, in his obtuse, unfaithful way, cared for her, otherwise he would have long since gone through with one of his oft-repeated threats to rid himself of her permanently. She was hard put to understand him at times, though; he continually made it appear that he would as soon she'd leave, yet if she gave the slightest indication of doing so, he got rough and clamped down.

Like earlier when she had asked Ledbetter about going to El Paso with him. Pete had made it plain she'd better forget it, and would have handed her one of his slaps if she'd been within reach. A bit of luck there for a change.

She didn't really mind the blows. They were never very hard and only stung for a few minutes. And later, when they were alone, Pete would say he was sorry and try to make up to her. He was a strange man, with an odd soft streak no one but she knew about — or even suspected. To the outside world he was as hard and ruthless as they came.

She had met Pete Vedic in Independence, where all the freighters and most of the wagon trains shaped up for the long trip West. He was an outrider then, looking for a job, and he'd got real interested in her, spending most of his time in the saloon where she worked.

Eventually they'd gotten together, and he'd finally persuaded her to move on with him — to the new country, as he called it. It was really opening up, he'd said, and there was plenty of opportunity for a good man. But later they'd found out that while the West was, in truth, opening up, there weren't many good jobs available.

And Pete was the kind who had big plans. He wanted to get ahead fast, and to do that he needed money. The next thing she knew he had it: plenty of gold and silver, along with a couple of hardcases who kept hanging around him all the time.

A day or two later she'd heard about a bank robbery. Three men. . . . Several thousand dollars in cash. . . . It had been a daring daylight holdup. Florinda had waited for the appropriate moment and then asked Pete point-blank about it.

He'd admitted it readily, saying that since there were no decent jobs to be had, and a man had to live, he'd taken the best way out. That was the way it had started.

Pete had grown fast in the business, soon became a well-known name who always, somehow, managed to elude the law while fattening his purse. Men drifted to him, begged to join his outfit. He'd turned away plenty of them. He was particular in that respect; he wanted only a special breed of men, like Pogue and Moon and Kansas, who took orders unquestioningly and followed them out to the last letter.

That, she supposed, was what made him a success. She smiled faintly at her use of the term. She could just see the looks on the faces of the folks back home if ever she told them her husband was a successful outlaw! But there was slim possibility of that. As far as they were concerned she had died the day she ran away with that drummer.

She stirred restlessly, got to her feet, and walked slowly to the jagged piece of mirror Melly had hung on the wall. Listlessly she tried again to arrange her hair, wished she had her packet of rouge and powder with her, but she'd left her room in such a fury, believing she'd find Pete with the girl, she hadn't given a thought to makeup.

Her thought of Melly brought the knife she had carried to her attention. It lay on the floor where it had fallen. She stared at it absently, wondered if she really would have used it if Ledbetter hadn't interfered, guessed maybe she would. She'd been pretty riled.

Discovering Ledbetter with the girl had really

surprised her. He didn't seem much interested in anything but gambling. She wasn't quite sure what to make of the tall man, and down deep he evoked a sort of uneasiness, a fear; it was like having a dark shadow fall across your path when he was around.

Pete evidently felt much the same. He treated Ledbetter like he was juggling eggs, careful to say only so much, go only so far, and not push — which wasn't Pete Vedic at all. Any other man blundering into the camp would have found himself back on the trail in a hurry — or dead.

She could see Pete wasn't anxious to cross Ledbetter — or the Widowmaker, as they said he was called. She supposed that was another example of how Pete was able to remain free and survive in a hostile world; he knew when to tread softly, and he used good judgment.

Well, maybe not always, to her way of thinking. This ransom deal he and Melly had cooked up, for one thing. She'd been against it from the start. It was too risky. Too many things could go wrong — it could even bring half a dozen U.S. marshals down on them. Sure, Pete had applied the usual caution, and it would be Les Brunkman who'd be in trouble if things went wrong. Or at least Pete had it figured that way.

Brunkman. . . . He was another of Pete's mistakes, far as she was concerned. It was too bad he hadn't let Ledbetter handle Les, blow his head off. It would have been better for everybody.

Pete wouldn't listen, but she kept telling him Brunkman was trying to take things over. One of these days —

Florinda's musings ceased abruptly as the door opened and the dark outline of a man filled the rectangle. It was not Pete Vedic, she knew instantly.

"Les!" she said, resentment and anger rising within her as always when they came together.

Scowling, Brunkman stepped into the room. He glanced around, brought his attention back to Florinda, considered her briefly with a kind of scornful tolerance.

"Where's Melly?"

"Gone."

"Gone!" he repeated. "Where?"

Florinda leaned back, eyes narrowing. Here, tailor-made, was a chance to rid herself and Pete Vedic of the man she feared and mistrusted.

"Afraid you've lost your little buttercup," she said slyly, deliberately goading him.

Brunkman's face darkened. "Who's she with? Not Pete — he's downstairs."

"You ought to be able to figure who —"

"Ledbetter!" Brunkman muttered. "That four-flushing son of a bitch — I'll —"

"Like to know where to find them?"

"You know?"

Florinda nodded, savoring each moment to its fullest. "Was me that sent them there. They wanted someplace private."

He took a long stride toward her, hand raised

to strike. "You — you lousy, stinking —"

Unflinching, she smiled up at him. "Maybe you ought to hurry. Might get there in time."

He caught himself. "Where are they?" he demanded in a savage voice.

"That old shack near the mine shaft. Take the trail —"

"I know where it is," he snapped, and spinning on his heel, hurried into the hall.

Florinda remained seated on the bed, listening to the quick thud of his boots as he went down the corridor. She heard the outside door squeak and then the protesting of the boards when he stepped onto the landing. A satisfied smile crossed her lips.

"I sure hope you picked out that tombstone, Les," she murmured.

15

Ledbetter, keeping Melanie Feak close to his side, picked his way through the trash and litter behind the old hotel, halted finally at its corner. Pressed by the need to get as far from the place in as short a time as possible, he looked anxiously for some indication of the stable.

Pogue had come from that direction, but the horses could be in any one of a half a dozen structures, scattered like sagging gray shadows through the darkness.

A horse stamped wearily. Aaron felt the pressure ease within him, and swung his eyes toward the source of the sound — a low, flat-roofed building fifty feet or so to the right.

"Come on," he murmured, and struck out immediately.

A few paces short he remembered Pogue and again stopped. Would he be there? It was doubtful; most likely he slept in the hotel with the others, but it wasn't worth taking a chance. Cautioning Melly, he drew his pistol and moved on in quiet, carefully placed steps.

They reached the entrance, a wide double-door arrangement, and he realized the building had been a barn for the convenience of the hotel's guests. Pausing just outside, Ledbetter listened intently. There was only the occasional stirring of a horse, the cheerful chirping of a cricket nestled somewhere in the rotting straw and dung.

Stepping through the doorway, he halted once more. If Pogue did choose to sleep near his charges, he'd likely be in the tack room to their left. Crossing over, Aaron peered into the small cubicle. The light from the moon was weak, but he was able to see clearly. There was no one there; Pogue was in the hotel.

He came around, glanced hurriedly along the runway. Sam Back's horse was in the first stall, with the gear slung across the separating half wall. He turned to the girl.

"Your horse — which one?"

She pointed to a dapple-gray farther down the line. Immediately he crossed to that stall, and hazing the animal to one side with his shoulder, began to throw on the saddle and bridle. He completed the chore hastily, with quick, efficient motions, and backed the dapple into the runway. Handing the reins to Melanie, he went then to the black and readied him.

Finished, he stopped beside the girl. "Those guards will still be on the road. Means we'll have to cut back through the hills, take a roundabout way. . . . Let's go."

Melanie didn't move. Ledbetter wheeled impatiently. In the subdued light her face was pale and set.

"Goddamn it — every second we stall around here —"

"I'm not going," she said.

Exasperation rocked Aaron Ledbetter. "The hell you're not!" he began, and then modified his tone. "What's got into you now?"

She shook her head. "Just not going back to Chacosa — or home, that's all. Either you take me straight on to El Paso, or I'll stay here."

"Told you we'd talk about it once we were in the clear."

Melanie looked directly at him. "I don't trust you," she said flatly. "I want an answer now."

It was best to try and reason with her — he'd learned that earlier. Brushing at the sweat clothing his brow, he said: "Got to go to Chacosa. Only way I can square myself with the marshal."

"Then I'm staying," she said stubbornly, dropping the dapple's reins.

"You still want that after what happened in your room tonight?"

"You mean Florinda?"

He nodded. "She wasn't playing games. She meant to kill you."

"I can take care of myself."

Aaron snorted his disgust. "You may think you can. You're just a green kid — a baby when it comes to dealing with people like her."

"I'm grown," Melanie said stiffly.

Somewhere back near the hotel gravel crunched. Ledbetter drew up sharply. It could

114

be someone coming, or just one of the outlaws, restless, out for a breath of fresh air. He rode out the dragging moments and then, when the sound did not come again, he turned to the girl.

"All right — I'll make you a proposition. We'll go to El Paso if you'll agree to one thing; we first swing by Chacosa, let the marshal —"

Melanie shook her head before he could finish. "You've said that — and I won't do it. I'll stay here, and when I get the money —"

A wave of frustration overcame Aaron. "The devil with it!" he rasped, abruptly fed up with bickering. He took a halfstep, swung a short blow to the girl's chin. Her head snapped back and she dropped soundlessly to the littered floor.

Moving fast, Ledbetter jerked his bandana from around his neck, placed it over Melanie's mouth, effectively gagging her. He disliked employing such tactics, but there simply wasn't time for argument.

Rolling her over, he bound her wrists behind her back and then considered the best way to place her on the saddle. She was limp, and he knew she would topple from the horse if he attempted to sit her upright.

There was only one answer. Hoisting her light body, he hung her over the saddle, secured her to either side with the buckskin thongs attached to the skirt. She began to stir at that moment, opened her eyes.

She stared wildly about, struggled violently against the tough leather strings. After a bit she gave it up. Ledbetter, gathering in the dapple's reins, grinned at her.

"If you'd showed sense, I wouldn't've had to do it the hard way."

She raged at him under the tight bandana, but he only shrugged and led the horse to where the black waited. He was up to his eyes with the whole fouled-up deal Sam Back had thrust upon him, and was wishing now he'd taken his chances before a judge. Never before had he gotten himself jockeyed into such a tight, and he was thoroughly sick of nursemaiding a silly kid of a girl bent on living a life she fancied was all glory and happy days.

He was fed up, too, with being forced to tread lightly in the presence of men whom he despised. That galled most of all. If and when he got Melanie Feak and the money back in Sam Back's hands, he just might delay that ride to El Paso long enough to settle a couple of scores.

Almost to the doorway, Aaron Ledbetter slackened his step. Impatience and exasperation again rushed through him; someone was there — or at least he thought he had heard something. . . . Goddam it, he was spooky as a burned bear. . . . If ever he allowed himself —

He came to a dead halt. He *had* heard something. He glanced around. He was in the center of the stable's runway, both horses and the again-struggling Melanie close behind him. There was no place to go.

Drawing his pistol, he started to pull back the

hammer, hesitated, eased it back into safety position. He'd be a fool to fire a shot; the noise would bring every man in the hotel down on his neck. Use the pistol as a club — that was all he could do, he realized, and once more cursed the luck that had placed him in such a disadvantageous position.

Ground reining the two horses, Aaron eased nearer to the doorway. The yard visible to him in front of the building, silvered by a pale moon, was empty; what brush he could see well appeared harmless enough, but he could look only into the forward fringe; beyond that lay deep shadows. He swore again in silent fury.

He reached the door and drew himself up close to the frame. Removing his hat, he peered around the corner. Nothing. . . . Once more he searched the dark areas beyond the yard, recognized nothing suspicious. Farther over, a portion of Lincoln Street was visible. It, too, was deserted.

Ledbetter settled back. The noise could have been caused by an animal of some kind — a mouse, or perhaps a rat. There were always plenty of both around old barns.

Holstering his weapon, he stepped back into the stable, took up the dangling reins of the horses. Casting a glance at Melanie, stonily quiet, he moved forward, mentally planning the course he'd take.

Turn sharp right once they were outside the building. Keep close to the wall where the shadows were deepest, just in case someone in the hotel happened to be looking in the direction of the barn . . . . Cross over fast, get into the brush and rocks as quickly as possible.

Once he'd gained that point, then mount up, and even though he'd be forced to take it slow since he'd be leading Melanie's dapple, it shouldn't take long to get a safe distance from the camp.

Gaining the doorway, Ledbetter paused momentarily, and then stepped into the open. Veering right, and holding the horses to short rein, he started across the front of the building

Almost to the corner he came to a stop. Les Brunkman, gun in hand and fury on his face, was waiting for him.

16

You — son of a bitch!" Brunkman snarled. "Running off with my woman —"

Ledbetter was a rigid shape in the moonlight. He stared coolly at Brunkman, calculating his chances of making a sudden move and drawing against an already-leveled gun — dismissed it when vague motion just beyond the squat outlaw caught his attention. A fraction of time later the small, wizened man he had earlier seen follow Brunkman from the hotel stepped into view. He, too, had his pistol ready.

"Who says she's your woman?" Ledbetter asked, stalling, not yet giving up entirely. "Seems I remember Pete —"

"Pete Vedic ain't running me!" Les cut in angrily. "Maybe he thinks so, but he ain't. Keep your hands up — away from that iron. Yancey there's just aching to tell folks how he filled you full of holes."

The sharp-faced little outlaw moved in closer. "Les — you told me —"

"Know what I told you!" Brunkman said impatiently. "Get that gun of his."

Yancey circled around, came in from behind Ledbetter and relieved him of his weapon. Melanie began to squirm and struggle against

119

her bonds. Brunkman glanced at her.

"Where was you headed? Seems she wasn't so keen on going."

Aaron only shrugged. He had transferred his attention to Yancey, seeking an opportunity there that would enable him to recover his weapon. But the slightly built man was eyeing him intently, and there appeared small chance. . . . Time — he needed time.

"Happens to be my business," he said.

Brunkman laughed. "Something you ain't got much of, you lousy tinhorn. I'm calling the shots now." He looked over his shoulder to Yancey. "Get the horses. We better be pulling out of here."

Yancey bobbed his head, and again circling wide, entered the barn. Les leaned back against the wall, cocked pistol pinning Ledbetter in his tracks.

"Pretty smart, letting Florinda think you was going up to that old shack, then heading straight for the horses. You in a big hurry?"

"Some," Aaron replied. "Better cut the girl loose."

Brunkman didn't move. "Things working out better'n I figured."

Ledbetter continued to watch the outlaw closely. He hoped none of the men in the hotel would put in an appearance; against Brunkman and Yancey he maybe stood a chance of making a break, but against Vedic and his entire gang it would be a different story.

"So?"

"Had made up my mind I'd have to forget the gal, and settle up with you some other time. Now I'll get the money and her — and square things with you, too."

"You double-crossing Pete Vedic?"

Brunkman grinned. "If you mean keeping that money I'll be collecting from her pa, and taking her, I reckon you could say I am."

Ledbetter shifted his weight, grunted. "You're a bigger fool than I thought."

Les bristled. "Better be watching your mouth —"

"He'll never let you get away with it."

"Can't do nothing about it. Time he figures out what's happened, I'll be halfway to Mexico."

"He won't give up that easy, and there's nothing says he can't follow you."

"How'll he know where I've headed?"

"Won't take him long to find out." Ledbetter paused, ducked his head at Melanie. "How about letting me cut her loose? No point keeping her tied down now."

"You keep standing right where you are," Brunkman warned, and then shook his head. "Expect leaving her that way's a right good idea — leastwise until we get far enough away from here so's nobody'll hear her holler. She was buttering up to Pete mighty strong."

"If you want to do the right thing you'll let her go on home. Hell, she's only a kid."

Les cocked his head to one side. "That what you was doing, letting her go?" He laughed, added, "Kid or not, she rode in here asking to be took in — and I'm just the bucko to do the taking."

Ledbetter once more shifted his weight. Brunkman studied him for a moment. Then, turning his head slightly, he called softly: "Hey, Yancey! You about ready?"

The outlaw's reply was unintelligible. Les, abruptly impatient, said, "Come on, hurry it up! We got to get out of here."

Ledbetter, continuing to spar for opportunity, took a casual step nearer Brunkman. "Big hole in that plan of yours. Pete'll be watching when you pick up that money."

"Won't even know it. He maybe'll try — only he'll be in the wrong place. I changed things, told Feak to meet me in Palisades Canyon 'stead of at the crossing like the note said."

Aaron wagged his head in mock admiration, ventured another cautious step. "Appears you set this thing up good."

"You're damn right I did. Ain't no sudden notion on my part. Been doing some scheming ever since this deal got started. Decided it was going to be me that cashed in this time, not Pete."

"Pulling out now like this — he'll know you're up to something."

"I ain't pulling out — not yet. Soon's I get the gal stashed back in the hills and take care of you, I'm coming back."

Ledbetter edged a third step closer. "Pete

Vedic's a lot smarter —"

"Hold it!" Les Brunkman barked, coming to strict attention. "Don't try easing in on me!"

Aaron settled back on his heels. Brunkman relaxed, grinned. "Sure, Pete's smart, but I'm a mite smarter. . . . And you doing all that fiddling around — you think I don't know what you're trying to do?"

Ledbetter shrugged. He had moved too fast, pushed too hard.

Les studied him for a moment. "Always heard you was a cool one. Reckon that much was right. Ain't you wondering what's going to happen to you?"

"Got a fair idea," Aaron said. "Only thing in my mind is if you're so damned set on getting rid of me, why drag me along? Why not do it now?"

"And wake up the whole bunch? Nope, I ain't that crazy. Besides, I don't want to be bothered none when I start working you over."

"I could make a run for it — force the play —"

"You won't. I know your kind. You'll play the odds, keep looking for a chance to jump me. But don't go worrying about it — I don't aim to kill you."

"Thought that was what you been looking for — a chance to notch my name on your gun."

Brunkman's eyes were bright, and the pale moonlight glistened on his sweaty face. "Got me a better idea. Time I'm done with you, you'll be wishing you was never born!"

Aaron remained silent. Brunkman leaned forward, a hard grin on his lips.

"Figured shooting was too good for you, Mister Widowmaker four-flusher. Too quick. You're going to do some squirming, because I'm going to bust up your hands so's you'll never pull a trigger again — then turn you loose. There'll be plenty just waiting to finish you off!"

Ledbetter's nerves tightened, but his features never changed. "You'll have to kill me first," he said quietly.

"I'm going to be real careful about that," Les said, and then looked up as Yancey came from the barn leading two horses.

The scrawny outlaw passed the reins of one to Brunkman, drew his pistol, and faced Ledbetter. Les nodded.

"Hold it on him — all the time, Yance. . . . I'll go first, lead the gal's horse. Put him following her. You come last, but keep up close. Understand?"

Florinda waited a full hour in Melly Feak's room for Pete to come, and then, rising, walked to the head of the stairs and looked down. He was still at the table, alone and drinking steadily. She considered him for a time, finally descended the splintered steps and crossed the empty saloon to where he sat.

He glanced up as she halted. His eyes were inflamed from the liquor, but it appeared to be having little effect on him otherwise. His capacity for drink had always been a marvel to her.

"What do you want?" he greeted sullenly.

"Time you come to bed," she replied, pulling up a chair. "Can't sit here all night."

"The hell I can't," he said morosely.

Florinda wiped out a glass, poured herself a small portion of whiskey. "Thought I'd tell you — no use stopping by that girl's room. She's gone."

He stared at her. "Gone where?"

"What's the difference? She's with Ledbetter."

Pete Vedic digested that slowly. "Ledbetter," he muttered. "Was anybody but him I'd —"

"You can forget about Les, too."

The outlaw pulled himself up straighter. "Les — what's he got to do with it?"

Florinda downed her drink. "He come looking for her. Told him where they were."

Vedic's eyes flared. His jaw sagged and he slammed his open hand upon the table hard, setting the glasses to rocking.

"You loco? Ledbetter'll kill him sure!"

"What I'm hoping," the blonde woman said calmly. "He's working against you, Pete. Has been all along. Told Fanny and some of the girls —"

"The hell with Fanny and the girls!" he shouted, his mouth working angrily. "You know what you've gone and done?"

"Maybe kept him from putting a bullet in your back —"

"You've messed up this deal with Feak real

good. Warned him to not pay off anybody but Les."

Florinda paled slightly. "I — didn't know —"

"Wasn't none of your goddamned business, so there ain't no reason you should!"

"You can send somebody else."

"Just got through telling you Les was the only one he's to give the money to. Somebody else shows up, Feak'll think something's wrong — probably back out. By God, I —"

Vedic choked on his words, pulled himself upright as rage tore through him. Eyes blazing, he leaned forward, shook a clenched fist in the woman's face.

"You better be praying nothing happens to Les! If Ledbetter kills him and I lose that five thousand dollars — you're going to be laying out there in that graveyard, right alongside him!"

17

They cut directly into the hills rising steeply behind Devil's Creek. After the first rise had been topped and the decaying structures of the mining camp were no longer visible, Yancey broke the quiet.

"Where we going, Les?"

Brunkman looked over his shoulder. "Don't be yelling like that. . . . We're heading for that old cabin on the ridge."

"Then what? Can't hang around there long. Vedic'll turn this country hindside to, hunting for us."

"You scared?" Brunkman asked in a sneering way.

"No, I ain't. Just like to know what you're figuring on doing. You changing plans all of a sudden's got me sort of mixed up."

"You do what I tell you and everything'll work out fine."

"Sure, but I still say it ain't smart to be waiting around —"

"Don't aim to — not for long, anyway. You and Melly'll hole up in the cabin while I go get the money. Quick as I'm back, we'll head south for Mexico."

Yancey nodded, satisfied. "What about him?"

he asked, pointing at Ledbetter.

"Changed my mind there, too. Tell you what I'm doing when we get to the cabin."

Aaron listened in bitter silence. Again he cursed the fates and Sam Back for putting him in such an untenable position — and with each passing moment it was growing worse. Somehow he had to make a break, escape before they reached the cabin Brunkman was taking them to. He turned, looked over his shoulder at Yancey. The wizened little outlaw grinned, waggled the pistol in his hand.

"Go ahead — try," he said invitingly.

Ledbetter swallowed his anger. . . . No chance there, Yancey was too anxious. . . . He'd have to find another way. He glanced at Melanie, a limp shape stirred only by the motion of her plodding horse. His eyes narrowed. Perhaps. . . .

"Telling you again," he called to Brunkman, "you better cut the girl loose. No good to you dead."

Immediately Les pulled aside, waited until Melanie's horse was abreast. "Hold up, Yance," he said, and dropped from the saddle. Moving to the girl's side, he drew a knife and sliced the rawhide pinning her down. She stirred weakly, began to slide. Brunkman caught her about the waist, stood her on her feet. Jerking the gag free, he peered into her face.

Swaying uncertainly, Melanie stared at him. Her eyes drifted to Ledbetter, to Yancey, came back finally to Les.

"Where —"

"You're all right," the outlaw said. "Ain't nothing to be worrying about."

She was having difficulty understanding, and Aaron guessed she had been only half conscious from the time they had ridden from the camp. . . . Or she could be smarter than he gave her credit for and was playing it dumb. He looked at the girl more closely.

"Where's — where's Pete and the others?" she whispered.

"Who gives a godamn about them?" Brunkman replied testily, obviously irritated. "I'm running things now."

"You?"

Les nodded. "Soon as I collect that money from your pa, we're lighting out for Mexico."

Melanie cast a surprised glance at Ledbetter. He moved his head slightly, verifying the outlaw's intentions.

"I see," she murmured, looking off across the hills.

Aaron studied the girl narrowly. There was a change in her, a nervousness — or perhaps it was fear. He gave that consideration; she had made a great show of wanting to become part of the outlaw gang, had insisted it was the only life for her, in fact. Was she now having second thoughts about it?

"Won't Pete know — hunt us down?"

Brunkman grinned, pleased at her apparent attitude. "I'll be watching out for you. Anyway, we'll be plenty far from here before he finds out. . . . We can live like rich folks in Mexico on five thousand dollars," he added as an afterthought.

"Be fine," Melanie said, and then turned her eyes to Ledbetter. "What about him?"

Brunkman made an offhand gesture. "Taking care of him soon's we get to the cabin."

She frowned. "You mean — kill him?"

"Not exactly. Just fixing it so's somebody can do it for me real easy. He's going to do plenty of sweating before he kicks in." Abruptly the outlaw paused, scowled. "Why? He mean something to you?"

"No — only murder —"

"Won't be murder, far as I'm concerned. Nothing for you to be stewing about, anyhow. You just keep busy being my woman, let me tend to everything else. Real important you remember that —"

"Kind of important we keep moving, too," Yancey said dryly. "We ain't so far from Pete Vedic's camp that we couldn't be spotted."

Brunkman threw a look to their back trail, spat. "Reckon you're right," he said, and reached for Melanie's arm. Helping her to the saddle, he grinned. "Guess this is what you been wanting, eh?"

She nodded, but Aaron had the feeling the answer was meant only to placate the outlaw, create time in which she hoped something — anything — could happen to free her from a predicament she no longer relished.

They rode on, climbing higher into the hills through the gray haze of coming dawn. Masses of golden crownbeard and other wild flowers covered the slopes and crowded the faint trail, and that together with an abundance of birds and small animals told Ledbetter they were in a remote, seldom-visited area.

They must be drawing near the cabin, he also realized, and the urgency to escape pressed harder upon him. His thoughts swung to Melanie and the problem she posed. Was he imagining a change in her? The uncertainty of it stirred him to irritability. He could be seeing something that wasn't actually there; it was best he not count on her.

To hell with all of them, he decided abruptly as the irritation gave way to harsh anger. He didn't care how she felt, or what she did. All he wanted was out of the tight he had been pushed into.

If he could manage to escape from Brunkman and the trigger-happy Yancey, he'd line out straight for El Paso, forget the whole deal. Let Sam Back find out for himself that the kidnapping was just a put-up job on the girl's part, that being with the outlaws was her own choice.

As for the future, he'd take his chances if the old lawman went through with his threats. Facing a judge and explaining his position would be a lot easier than trying to save a girl who didn't want saving, and maybe getting himself—

"Here we are," Les Brunkman sang out as

131

they broke from the brush and entered a small clearing. He grinned at Melanie. "Going to be home for a couple hours or so," he added and winked broadly.

"The bridal soot," Yancey said, and laughed.

Ledbetter was only half listening. The cabin, he noted, was low and built of stone, apparently had served as quarters for some miner in years past. The windows were little more than ports, and it looked to have but one door. Escape from such a place would be virtually impossible.

They filed into the yard and drew up before a sagging hitch rail. Immediately Brunkman, gun in hand, wheeled to cover Ledbetter. He motioned to Yancey.

"Toss a couple of loops over him," he said, "and snub him up tight to one of them big trees. Then see if you can find me a singlejack, or maybe an axe or a hammer."

Grinning, Yancey dropped from his horse. Brunkman nodded to Aaron. "You're first on the program, Mister Four-flusher. Aim to get you out of the way right quick, so's I can have some time with my bride before I go calling on her pa."

18

Yancey smirked, reached for the lariat hanging from his saddle. Pulling it loose, he shook out a loop and turned toward Ledbetter. Aaron eyed the outlaw coldly, steeled himself for a desperate break. Brunkman would have to shoot him; he'd never let them cripple his hands.

"Oh —"

Melanie's sudden cry brought them all about. The girl had slumped, was falling from her horse — whether by intent or not Ledbetter had no idea. He was sure of only one thing — the opportunity he had sought was presenting itself.

Jerking the black horse around savagely, he brought him into collision with Yancey. The outlaw yelled and went sprawling to the ground as the black, hurdling him, plunged for the brush a dozen strides away.

Les Brunkman shouted an oath, fired hastily. The bullet clipped foliage only inches from Aaron's head as he ducked into the thicket. He veered sharply, expecting more shots, but none came.

Bent low, he held the black to a reckless run over the uneven terrain for a hundred feet or so, again changed course to the opposite direction. He could hear someone coming, wondered

133

which of the outlaws it would be. Brunkman, likely, as he had been in the saddle.

Ledbetter rushed on, soon felt the black begin to tire under him as they bulled their way blindly through the tangle of scrub oak and thorny locusts. He'd be forced to slow down shortly and allow the black to catch his wind, or he'd stumble and go down sure. And that would be fatal; on foot, with no weapon, he was defenseless and at the mercy of the outlaws.

Aaron glanced toward the higher slopes. The brush continued in a somewhat narrow strip running well up into one of the numerous canyons that gashed the hillside. If he could swing off, get into the canyon, there was a good chance he might throw whoever was pursuing him off his trail. . . . And chances were equally good, he realized grimly, that he would be placing himself in a trap.

But the need to do something immediately was paramount; sooner or later Brunkman would catch a glimpse of him and the faltering black, and open up. At such short range he would be an easy target.

Coming to a decision, he swung the black to the right, going into a dense stand of piñon and juniper trees interwoven with white flower clumps of buckbrush. The horse dropped to a labored walk on the steeper grade, and Aaron did not press him, aware that the noise of his passage had instantly diminished.

Ledbetter heard then the sounds of the man

behind him, halted quickly in a leafy screen to watch. It was Les Brunkman, as he had expected. The outlaw was looking straight ahead, holding the reins high in his left hand, while in the right a cocked pistol was in firing position.

Brunkman's face was flushed and angry. Evidently he had become aware of the cessation of noise ahead of him, and wary of ambush, was proceeding with caution. The outlaw moved by, disappeared into the heavy growth.

Ledbetter remained where he had halted, considered his next move while the black gradually recovered his spent wind and the trembling of his body faded. He could not remain there. Les would soon realize he had bypassed his quarry, double back and search the only area into which he could have turned — the canyon.

Aaron raised himself in the stirrups, threw his glance to either side of the narrow slash. The brush thinned out along the edges, and both slopes offered little concealment should he elect to pull directly out of the declivity.

His best bet was to backtrack, attempt to get beyond the outlaw, possibly behind him, and follow at a safe distance. If he could keep Brunkman ahead, and thus change the order of things, become the pursuer instead of the pursued, he stood a better chance of coming out of the encounter alive.

And he wouldn't have to engage in the deadly game of hide-and-seek for long. Brunkman would be forced to abandon the hunt shortly; his meeting with Feak was set for mid-morning, now only a few hours away. All he need do was be careful, keep out of sight.

Once Les gave up and headed back, that would be it, Aaron vowed silently. He would be out of it. He'd cut down the mountain and head south, not risk swinging by Chacosa at all. As far as the black horse was concerned, he'd arrange for an exchange later. Important thing was he'd be through with the whole fouled-up mess — clear of Brunkman, Vedic, Melanie Feak, Sam Back, and all.

Taking a final look at the area into which Les had disappeared, he wheeled the black around and started down the slope and out of the canyon. He held the horse to a slow, quiet walk. There was no need for speed, only for care.

He reached the mouth of the canyon and pulled up to listen. He could hear nothing. He wondered if the outlaw had moved beyond range or, like him, had stopped to listen.

He grunted his annoyance, cursed again the luck that had placed him in a position where he was forced to run and hide. It rubbed against the grain, and he mentally vowed to provide himself with a hideaway gun in the future — assuming there was a future.

He remained at the edge of the canyon for a full five minutes, still hearing nothing. Deciding then that it was risky to delay longer, he once more put the black into motion, and moved forward onto the brush-covered flat.

Abruptly he halted. Somewhere off to his right he caught the muted *tunk-a-tunk* of an approaching horse. Brunkman! It was too late to fade back into the canyon, too late to move at all. He was trapped. Rigid, he waited out the dragging moments.

He couldn't determine the exact location of the outlaw, only that he was drawing close. Knotting the black's reins, he hooked them over the saddle horn, pulled his feet back until only the toes of his boots were in the stirrups. If he were forced to jump, he wanted to be in position to do so quickly.

Movement in the depths of the brush slightly behind him caught the tail of his eye. He dared not turn his head, aware the slightest motion could attract. The dull thud of Brunkman's horse on the packed leaves and litter became more pronounced. Aaron felt his nerves tighten, his muscles bunch.

And then the sound was passing to the rear of him, the quiet thump of hooves, the faint squeak of leather, the swish of disturbed brush.

Ledbetter forced himself to remain still while he hoped the black would not stamp or stir impatiently for another few moments. His luck held. The careful noise lessened, faded entirely. Aaron took a deep, grateful breath, turned on the saddle. The outlaw had passed not twenty feet away.

He swung the black around, and keeping deep

in the brush, looked to the direction into which Brunkman had ridden. Surprise touched him. Les was passing up the canyon, was heading instead for the cabin. Apparently he was giving up the chase, deciding it was more important to meet with Feak than run down and exact the vengeance he felt was due him.

Removing his hat, Aaron mopped at the sweat accumulated on his forehead. It had been close — but that was it. It was over with now — finished. He could go his way and leave Brunkman and the others to their own affairs. He'd been lucky; all it had cost him was time — and his gun.

The latter irked him considerably. He'd carried the Colt's with its coin-inlaid handles for quite a spell, and its smooth, faultless action was as familiar to him as the sky above. But it wasn't worth risking his neck for. A man could always obtain another pistol, and with a little time and effort, hone it to the perfection he had attained with that particular one.

He started to turn away, strike south, paused. . . . Melanie . . . what about her? If he moved on, washed his hands of the deal, he'd be leaving the girl to the mercy of Les Brunkman. But that was what she wanted — or at least *had* wanted. Ledbetter frowned; he wasn't so dead sure now.

He thought he had noted a change in her, almost a fear of Brunkman, in fact. And back at the cabin — had she actually fainted or intentionally created a diversion to permit his escape?

The latter was possible, he told himself, and if true, running out on her now wouldn't be right.

Ledbetter stirred angrily, impatient with his disturbing thoughts, with the indecision that gripped him. He could be wrong about her. Perhaps he should just ride on, forget it. Melanie had said she sought escape from a humdrum life — and certainly had made it appear that way. If he went back he could be doing it for nothing, and at the possible expense of his own life.

But he couldn't be sure, and Aaron Ledbetter realized he'd never be able to live with himself if he didn't actually know.

He glanced to the north, probed the long slopes for several moments. Finally he caught sight of Les Brunkman topping out the last rise. Aaron gauged the sun. The outlaw would be riding on to keep his rendezvous with Everett Feak, leaving Yancey and Melanie at the cabin. At least, that had been his plan; likely there'd be no change.

He'd give Les a quarter hour and then follow. Once at the cabin he'd figure a way to overcome Yancey and free the girl — if that was what she wanted. And as for recovering Ev Feak's money, that would be up to Sam Back.

Then for damn sure he'd head south.

19

How'd it happen, Marshal?"

Sam Back gingerly touched his head and thought: *No sense in that Ledbetter hitting me so goddamn hard.* He lowered his eyes, then straightened and faced the dozen or so townspeople gathered in his office.

"Tricked me, that's what he done. Ain't going to deny it, he tricked me good."

"But the keys — how could he —"

"Was this way," the lawman said, leaning against his desk. "Was setting here going over some papers when this Ledbetter started groaning something awful. Started hollering for me, so I got up and went to his cell. Told me he had a terrible bellyache."

"Wasn't you suspicious of him?"

"Sure I was, but he made it look real good, so I went and got the keys, figuring to take a look at him before I went for the doc. Well, second I opened that door and stepped inside, I knew I'd made a mistake.

"He come off'n that cot quicker'n a greased cat. He's a quick one, that Ledbetter. Then he hit me a smart one over the head, knocked me cold almost before I knew what was going on. When I come to a bit later he'd gone."

140

"On your horse," a man finished, with a laugh.

Sam nodded despondently, stared at the floor. . . . Let them laugh now — his time would come later, and they'd be eating their snide remarks and choking on their chuckles. What they didn't know was that he was sitting in this game with a big ace in the hole — an ace in the form of Aaron Ledbetter, the deadliest gunman of them all.

"That when you got the posse together and tried following him?" someone else asked.

"Thereabouts. Henry Dooley showed up, yelling he'd seen Ledbetter heading north. He figured something was wrong, so he come to see just what. Then's when we got the posse going."

The old lawman paused, brushed at his mustache. He could feel the excitement in the hot, stuffy room, and he was making the most of it.

"Couldn't muster but two more citizens, outside us, willing to ride, but we went anyway. Trailed Ledbetter far as we could. Didn't turn back till we seen he was heading into Vedic's hideout. I sure wasn't about to let them boys with me get all shot to hell wading into that bunch — forted up the way they are."

"What's next, then?" Harvey Kitchell demanded, his face showing worry. "You dropping it there? Like to know because my bank's not safe anymore, all things considered. Seems to me we ought to be calling in a U.S. Marshal, or maybe the Army."

"No need for that," Sam said quickly. "Just you leave everything to me."

141

"But you said a posse wouldn't have a chance —"

"Know I did, and it wouldn't. But one man by hisself can turn the trick."

There was a dead silence in the room. Kitchell looked around with a stunned expression. "You mean you're aiming to try —"

"Just exactly what I mean. I'll collar Ledbetter and get the girl back, too. What's more, I'll —"

"Girl?" a surprised voice said. "What girl?"

Sam Back shrugged. "Well, reckon there ain't no point keeping it quiet no longer. Ev Feak's daughter's been kidnapped by Vedic and his bunch. Sent a letter to Ev telling him if he didn't fork over five thousand dollars he'd never see her again."

"Five thousand dollars!" someone exclaimed with a low whistle. "Where in hell will Ev get that much money?"

The lawman flung a scornful glance at Kitchell. "Not from the bank, for sure. Harvey told him he couldn't help. Ev finally talked this brother of his into making a loan. Expect he mortgaged hisself for the rest of his natural life."

"Poor old Ev. . . ."

"Figure to get the money back for him, too," the marshal said confidently. "Ev's paying off this morning. I'll be there, watching and waiting."

"Alone?" a man asked in an incredulous voice.

"Yessir, alone. Deal like this it's always best to work by yourself."

"But you can't do no good — one man against a dozen hardcases!"

"Can't do no good with a whole bunch tramping around, upsetting things. Matter like this'n has got to be handled quiet and easy. Figure I can move in, do what's needed doing, and get out — fast."

As if not certain he had heard right and wanted to be sure, Harvey Kitchell leaned forward. "You saying you're going in there, get Feak's daughter, recover the money, and recapture your prisoner — all by yourself?"

"Just what I said."

Again there was total quiet. Finally someone in the center of the crowd said: "My God, Sam, that's a powerful big chore!"

"Know it," the marshal said soberly, "but it's my job. What you all hired me to do."

"But — alone?"

"I can do it. And I sure don't want nobody trying to help. Just mess things up. Now, get out of here, all of you. I got work to do."

"Maybe if a few of us was to ride out —"

"Be the wrong thing. Go on about your business, and pass the word along — there ain't nobody to go out on the north road until I'm back. Understand? Nobody! If there's shooting I don't aim to have nobody killed by a stray bullet like Amos Greene was. Expect I'll have the whole thing cleared up by dark."

"What if you haven't?" Kitchell asked bluntly.

The old lawman looked out of the dusty

window to the sun, now well started on its climb into the heavens. *Jackpot or nothing!* he thought, and turned to face the skeptical banker.

"If I don't," he said firmly, "then I reckon I'd best hand over my badge and let you folks find yourselves a lawman who can do the job right for you."

20

Ledbetter reached the edge of the clearing in which the cabin stood. He could see only the rock chimney of the structure because of the somewhat higher level, and immediately cut back, planning to circle and approach from the rear. He wasn't sure what to expect of Melanie; she could simply be waiting with Yancey for Brunkman's return — or she could be a prisoner.

Gaining a point at the back of the squat building, he walked the black in close as he dared and dismounted. Tying the horse to a dwarf pine, he moved forward on foot, taking his time and making no sound.

He worked out of the screening brush at the upper end of the cabin's rear. Glancing around to assure himself that Yancey was nowhere in the weedy fringe that bordered the clearing, he darted across a narrow strip of open ground and came up against the stone wall.

Ledbetter paused there and listened intently. Hearing nothing, he edged toward the small window to his right and peered in. The door, directly opposite, was open, permitting a small amount of light to enter the gloomy square. By shifting himself about he was able to examine all but the area immediately below the window. A crude table, a cook stove, a bunk built against the wall — but no sign of Melanie or Yancey.

The latter he could explain; his portion of the yard fronting the hut was restricted to that visible through the doorway. Yancey, conceivably, could be just outside, sitting on a bench Aaron had noted earlier.

Melanie could be with him. He was still convinced that Brunkman had not changed his plan, that the two would be there awaiting his return.

Frowning, he started to pull back, caught himself sharply. A faint scraping sound, as a boot or shoe scuffing against the floor, reached him. He crowded closer, endeavored to see the base of the wall below the window. The opening was too small, and after a few moments he gave it up.

But Aaron was sure now; Melanie was inside, apparently bound and gagged. He settled back, gave that thought. Had the girl actually indicated an unwillingness to accompany Les Brunkman when he returned with the money? Was she a prisoner?

Or was it a carefully laid trap to ensnare him when he came back seeking the girl? And where was Yancey? Had he ridden on with Brunkman, leaving the girl trussed and helpless to await the outlaw's convenience? If so, they were not expecting him.

His thoughts were moving too fast. . . . Yancey could be out front, standing guard just as expected; binding Melanie could be just a precaution.

There was only one way to find the answer. Turning, he wormed his way carefully across the rear of the cabin, rounded the corner, and continued along its side until he reached the forward edge. Pushing aside a clump of brush slanting against the stone wall, he looked into the yard.

It was deserted. Yancey was not to be seen, nor were the horses. Tension began to prick at Ledbetter's nerves. What the hell was the score? Keeping well behind the thick foliage of the shrub, he spent a full five minutes probing the undergrowth beyond the weed fringe. Nothing. . . . Either Yancey had accompanied Brunkman to keep the meeting with Feak, or he was expertly hidden.

Aaron glanced at the sun. Time was slipping by fast. Brunkman — and Yancey, if they were together — would be returning soon. If he — the thought came to him suddenly; Melanie's horse. If the girl had been left there by the outlaws for safekeeping until they completed their business, her horse would still be around. It came to him then, just as quickly, that this was a trap prepared for him.

He drew himself up stiffly. He'd wondered about Melanie, wondered if she'd actually changed her thinking about going with the outlaws. Apparently she had, although he wouldn't put it past Brunkman to make use of her in any way that suited his purpose, agreeable to her or not.

Ledbetter gave that thought, again considered

climbing aboard his horse and pulling out, leaving it all behind. He dismissed the inclination with a shrug. There was but one thing he could do; get to Melanie, release her, and try to get past Yancey, who'd probably show himself once he saw Aaron enter the cabin.

Yancey wouldn't shoot, he was fairly certain of that. Les had taken it in mind to exact revenge for wrongs he fancied had been visited upon him, and likely had instructed the small-sized outlaw not to use his weapon unless forced.

Aaron realized he'd have to chance it, regardless. Wasting no more time, he bent forward, gathered his muscles, and spurting suddenly from the brush at the corner, raced for the open doorway.

He reached it, ducked inside. Then — and only then — did a gunshot rap through the warm hush lying over the hills, and a bullet ring sharply against the rock wall. The slug hadn't been meant to hit him; it was only Yancey's way of telling him he'd walked into a trap and that it had been sprung.

Not bothering to close the split log door, Ledbetter crossed to where Melanie lay. A folded bandana, his own, was tied across her lips. Ankles and wrists had been linked together with rawhide strings.

Drawing his knife, he slashed the cords and then removed the gag. He looked at her closely in the murky light.

"You all right?"

The wildness began to fade from her eyes. She nodded weakly, rubbed at her chafed wrists. "I — I was afraid you'd not come back —"

All the bravado, the self-assurance and determination he had seen in the hotel at Devil's Creek were gone; he thought for a moment she was going to break down, go to pieces.

"Now maybe you'll listen to me!" he snarled, deliberately harsh in an attempt to jar her, bring her around.

Melanie's head came up. Fire flashed briefly in her eyes. "You don't need —"

He rose, wheeled away, ignoring her last words, his mind already facing the problem next at hand. Crowding up close to the door, he looked out. Yancey had forsaken his hiding place, was now in the clearing a few paces away and in position to observe the cabin with ease. The outlaw saw Ledbetter, grinned broadly.

"Welcome back — sucker."

Yancey squatted on his heels. He had his pistol out, was holding it half raised in his right hand. Aaron studied him thoughtfully; best he let the twisted little man think he was holding the whip — as indeed he was, Aaron noted wryly — until he could figure out a plan for escape.

Make him feel confident, perhaps become a bit careless. But there wasn't much time left to play around with. At that moment Brunkman was probably at the designated place, meeting with Feak — or he could be starting the return trip to the cabin.

"You're calling the shots," he said. "What comes next?"

Yancey toyed with his pistol. "Just settle back. Les'll be along pretty soon."

A while earlier Pete Vedic, leaning against the splintered frame of the hotel doorway, watched Brunkman ride into the yard and pull up to the hitchrack. Relief and satisfaction trickled through him; Ledbetter hadn't shot the damned fool's head off; why, he didn't know and didn't care. Important thing was that Les was still alive.

Turning, he looked beyond the half a dozen men standing behind him in the lobby entrance to Florinda, poised at the foot of the stairs. He saw the stiff lines of worry slip from her face, saw her shoulders go down as she moved deeper into the saloon. She'd learned her lesson, he guessed. Be a long time before she stuck her nose in his business again.

"Want to talk to you when I get back," he heard Les say, and came around to meet the younger man.

"About what?"

Brunkman slouched on the saddle. "I ain't been fooled none by all this fancy jigging you been doing. Way you got it set up, you ain't taking none of the chances in this ransom deal. Nobody knows you're mixed up in it 'cause you ain't put your name to nothing."

Vedic regarded Les unblinkingly. "So?"

"Since I'm the bucko taking all the risk, I got a

bigger share coming."

Florinda was right about him, Vedic thought. *Tried to tell me Les was out for himself, that he'd cross me someday.*

"What risks?" he asked lazily.

"There'll be aplenty! What if that jasper brought along a U.S. Marshal? Might even have a posse hiding back in the brush."

And you got something stirring around in that head of yours, Les boy. You're putting on a show, trying to finagle me. Only I ain't finagling. I'm a jump ahead of you.

"There won't be no law or no posse," the outlaw leader said. "Feak wants that girl of his back."

Brunkman shook his head. "All we're going on is what she told us. Could be he'll be glad to get rid of her."

"Ain't likely. . . . Anything else?"

Brunkman was doing his utmost to maintain a strong facade in the face of Vedic's laconic manner. He shrugged.

"Nope, reckon not. Just figured we ought to have ourselves this here little understanding. . . . Supposing Feak don't have the money?"

"He'll have it," Pete Vedic said.

"But what if he don't?"

"Then you come trotting back and tell me," the outlaw said dryly. "Now, move out. Getting late."

Brunkman touched his horse with spurs, wheeled about. He was unsure just how he had come off in the exchange. He had a feeling that somehow Vedic had made a fool of him — but the last verse hadn't been sung yet, he thought smugly. Twisting on the saddle, he looked back.

"You be waiting here, like we planned?"

Vedic's smile was humorless. "Like we planned. Why?"

"Only wanted to be sure," Les said, and swung off into Lincoln Street.

Vedic's round eyes didn't shift from Brunkman until the man reached the corner and dropped from sight. Then he looked down. He'd have to admit it, he thought again. Florinda had been right about Les all along. And looking back, she'd been right about a lot of things. He guessed he ought to tell her so, make her feel good. Hell, he might even marry her some day — he'd tell her that, too. But first he'd better get things to moving. Wouldn't do to let Brunkman work himself up too big a lead. He looked over his shoulder.

"All right, boys. Get the horses."

21

Ledbetter turned back into the shadowy depths of the cabin. Outside Yancey rose, and swaggering a bit in the boots that seemed sizes too large for him, moved to the hitchrack and leaned against the rail. He was twirling his pistol around on a forefinger.

Aaron glanced about the room, desperate now for a weapon, an idea — anything that would effect an escape. Les Brunkman likely was well on his return trip by this time, and once he arrived, hope for Melanie and himself would be slim.

His gaze settled on the girl. She stood, back to the wall, watching him with frightened eyes. She appeared very young now, despite the ridiculous dance-hall-girl dress she wore, and far from the outlaw woman she had planned to become.

"Is there anything I can do?" she asked in a hesitant voice.

His temper was short. "Just stay put — out of the way," he snapped, angry with her, with himself, with all things in general.

How could he have gotten himself into a situation like this? Trapped in a cabin, weaponless, with a slip of a girl who meant absolutely nothing to him — and about to die at the hands of a man he scarcely knew and certainly had no quarrel with!

Some joke — cashing in this way! He'd expected it someday when he'd run up against a man faster than himself with a gun, and had long ago accepted the inevitability of that event. But this. . . .

He grinned crookedly, swore. Melanie raised her head hopefully. He spun impatiently away, resumed his search of the room. Moving in front of the doorway, he halted. Yancey was engaged in a minute inspection of his weapon, which appeared to be new.

If there was only some way of getting the wiry little outlaw into the cabin, or even within arm's reach, there might be a chance he could trick him, gain possession of the gun. He shrugged away the thought. Yancey was wary; he'd remain right where he was, never fall for any yarn that would put him in danger.

Ledbetter began his restless cruising again, now and then brushing at the sweat continually gathering on his forehead. He had no specific idea as to what he might find, knew only that he must procure something he could employ as a weapon. Perhaps something that would resemble a pistol or a rifle — a rod, a bar — even a round piece of wood of proper size. Anything was worth taking a chance with now — anything.

He paused by the stove, sat down on its flat surface to think. As he rested his hand on the cool metal his fingers traced the circular edge of a lid. Instantly he came upright. Lifting one of the iron plates by the nubs in its handle indentation, he took it between thumb and forefinger, swung it experimentally.

Hope rose within Aaron. It might work. Yancey was less than thirty feet distant. The lid, sailed with all the force he could muster, would be a lethal weapon if it struck its intended target squarely. And if not, it might prove distraction enough to put the outlaw within his grasp.

Holding the lid behind him, he moved back until he was standing directly in front of the open doorway, but slightly toward the rear of the cabin. Still in pursuit of proficiency, Yancey was twirling his weapon by the trigger guard. The outlaw did not look up.

Ledbetter nodded his satisfaction. Yancey was unable to see movement inside the shack unless it was near the doorway. He could position himself, therefore, where the possibility of accuracy with the iron lid was at its best. Recrossing the room, he showed the plate to Melanie.

"I'll try to hit him with this. If I'm lucky, he'll go down. Regardless, the instant I throw it I aim to go through that door and jump him."

Melanie, understanding, smiled faintly. Aaron looked again at the outlaw.

"When I do, you wait ten seconds, then run for the horses. Know where they are?"

"In the brush. On the other side of the yard."

"Get on yours quick, and get out of here. Know the way home?"

"Yes, but can't I help —"

He shook his head. "Only way you can is to get away fast. Brunkman's due any minute."

She looked down, and he thought he saw her tremble slightly. "You'll be fine," he said in a gentler tone. "Ready?"

"Ready," she murmured, and then added, "Want to thank you for coming back — for helping me."

"Forget it. Important thing is you woke up before it was too late. Life you're looking for is not with men like Vedic or Brunkman." He paused, said as if it were an afterthought, "Or me. No future in it."

She sighed heavily. "No future for me in anything."

"That'll change. Just be satisfied — and patient." He glanced at Yancey. "Best we hurry."

Melanie nodded, stepped back out of the way. Aaron moved to a position in the center of the room and to one side of the doorway. Taking a firm grip on the stove lid, he took what aim was possible, and putting everything he had into it, hurled the iron plate straight at the outlaw.

Yancey glanced up, saw it coming — but too late. He yelled and tried to leap aside. The lid caught him, edge forward, high on the chest. He stumbled back, fell hard.

Ledbetter was through the doorway and on him almost before he was on the ground. Yancey yelled again, began to scream curses as he tried to bring his pistol into use. Ledbetter slapped him hard across the eyes, seized the pistol by the barrel. Wrenching it free, he swung hard, using it as a club.

The heavy weapon thudded into the outlaw's skull. He went limp instantly. Aaron, breathing hard from his efforts, leaped to his feet and glanced around. Melanie was just emerging from the brush at the edge of the clearing. She was on her horse and leading Yancey's.

He started across the yard to meet her, angry because she had not fled as he had directed, thankful that she'd had the presence of mind to bring him the outlaw's horse.

Snatching the reins from her, he vaulted to the saddle and wheeled for the brush beyond the cabin where the black waited. Looking over his shoulder, he saw that she was following close. They reached the undergrowth behind the shack, veered toward his horse.

Reaching down, he jerked the black's reins clear, and leading him, spurred across the slope. He'd stay on Yancey's mount for a short distance and then change to the black. There was no time for such now.

He glanced back again. Melanie was only a length away. She smiled, and he answered with a grin. They'd made it.

22

When Brunkman broke out of the trees on the lip of Palisades Canyon, he saw Ev Feak's red-wheeled buggy waiting far below at the fork in the trail. Grinning, he started down the slope. He'd played it smart, changing the meeting place from Bear Paw Crossing to the canyon. If Pete Vedic planned to keep an eye on him, he'd be watching the wrong place.

He reached the bottom of the grade. Scanning the surrounding area with sharp, suspicious eyes, he walked his horse slowly toward the rancher. He didn't think Feak was fool enough to try any tricks, but a smart man always took everything into consideration and avoided risks when possible.

The rancher's features revealed the strain he was under. He leaned forward, called anxiously: "Where's my daughter? Said you'd turn her over to me when I brought the money."

Brunkman pulled to a halt alongside the vehicle. He smiled, finding some sort of sick enjoyment in the man's misery. "You got the cash?"

Feak reached down to the floorboards, picked up a canvas sack, hefted it. "Right here. Coin and paper, just like you told me. . . . Is

Melanie all right?"

"Sure. She's in good shape," Les said, taking charge of the sack.

Settling back on the saddle, he untied the strings that closed the bag, probed through its contents. After a few moments he raised his eyes to the rancher.

"You goddamn sure there's five thousand here? If there ain't —"

"It's all there!" Feak cried in a wild voice. "For God's sake, man — what about my little girl? Where is —"

"She'll be along," the outlaw replied. "Soon as I'm on my way and I know you ain't up to some cute trick."

"I ain't!" the rancher protested. "Come alone, and I done just exactly like you told me. I wouldn't try tricking you — not with my daughter's life at stake."

"That's being smart," Brunkman said. "Now, you just set quiet while I. . . ."

The outlaw's voice trailed off into silence. Three men, each carrying a rifle, had broken from the brush. They approached slowly, swinging around to box him in. He turned his angry eyes to Feak.

"You goddamn lying —"

"I don't know nothing about them!" the rancher shouted, his face reflecting the shock and surprise that gripped him. "Before God I don't!" He turned to the rider coming in on his left. "Carter, why'd you do this? I gave my word

159

— promised I wouldn't bring nobody. You know that!"

Carter Feak was a few years younger than his brother and resembled him not at all. His features were grim.

"Figured I'd better keep tabs on you," he told Feak, staring at Brunkman. "Good thing I did. You're throwing that money away."

Les Brunkman listened, a cold smile on his lips. He ducked his head in the direction of Carter. "Who's this jasper?"

"My brother. You've got to believe me — I didn't know he'd be here. . . . Was him loaned me the money."

"I'll be taking it back," the younger Feak said quietly.

Brunkman looked around casually. One of the rancher's men faced him from beyond the buggy, rifle leveled. The second covered him from the side. He gave them bitter appraisal, shrugged.

"Reckon you know what this means," he said, turning back to Everett Feak. "Deal's off."

The rancher leaped from his buggy, hurried to the outlaw's side. "No — you can't say that! Wasn't my fault they showed up — wasn't supposed to." He wheeled, rushed to where his brother sat in stony silence. "You got to get out of here, leave me be! Please!"

Carter continued to stare at Les. "The girl still alive?"

Brunkman nodded. "Good as new — only she

160

won't be if I don't get back there pretty quick with this money. Boys are just hoping there won't be no payoff. Heard them cutting cards for her last night."

Ev Feak's features blanched, and his lips formed into a soundless cry. Clawing at Carter's arm, be managed one word. "Please —"

The younger Feak shook his head. "You're a fool, Ev, taking an outlaw's word for anything."

"What else can I do? What choice I got? It's Melanie, my own flesh and blood I'm bargaining for!"

Brunkman, in complete control of the moment, cocked his head to one side. "What's it going to be? I'm getting tired of setting here. . . . Make up your mind."

"Take the money — go!" Ev Feak shrilled, turning his back on his brother. "Only thing that counts is my daughter."

Les shifted his attention to Carter. "You feeling the same?"

The younger brother was silent for a long moment, and then finally shrugged. "Take it," he said. Turning, he touched the two riders with a tired look. "Let him go, boys."

Brunkman's mouth pulled into a hard grin. Twisting around, he stuffed the sack of money into his saddlebags, taking time to buckle the flap securely. That completed, he squared himself on the saddle.

"*Adiós,*" he said, and touching the brim of his hat, swung about and started up the slope.

There was nothing but contempt in Les Brunkman for the men watching him depart. The poor suckers — like all honest-johns, they were helpless when you handled them tough. He displayed his utter scorn by not even bothering to look back.

Pete Vedic, after scattering the three men who had accompanied him along the upper end and opposite side of Palisades Canyon, turned his attention to the scene below. Earlier they had followed Brunkman from the hotel at a safe distance, had watched him ignore the trail to Bear Paw Crossing and continue east for the canyon. It was apparent then to the others that Vedic, as usual, was right; Les was double-crossing them.

"It's that goddamn girl," Kansas had said as they rode off to take their assigned positions, calculated to head Brunkman off regardless of the direction he took. "Got him rocking on his heels. You sure had him figured, Pete."

Vedic had made no comment, had simply watched Les moving down the slope. He felt old and tired, realized suddenly he could no longer go without a night's sleep. But it didn't affect his brain any, he guessed; he could still outsmart the best of them.

Hooking one leg over the saddle horn, he watched as Feak handed the sack of money to Brunkman. He'd figured the rancher would come through. Kids were a man's soft spot. You really hit him where it hurt when you grabbed one of them. . . . He guessed he'd feel the same way if, someday, he and Florinda had a kid. He smiled faintly, considering that. He and Florinda with a kid! The smile faded. Maybe it wasn't so far-fetched after all.

Vedic sat up straighter. Three men had ridden out of the brush, were closing in on Brunkman with leveled rifles. He leaned forward, studied them more closely. They weren't lawmen; at least, they weren't wearing badges. He settled back. Friends of Feak, he guessed, trying to give him some help. Only like most well-meaning friends, they'd made the wrong move at the wrong time.

He wasn't worried. Les could take care of himself. And Feak and his friends, whoever they were, couldn't afford to nab Les or interfere in any other way. That the rancher had shown up with the money was proof he wanted his daughter back. He'd let nothing jeopardize the exchange.

Besides, Les was smart. He always used his head when he got in a tight — and he always came out on top. Too bad he was smart the wrong way; too bad he'd gone and got big ideas of his own. It was going to kill him.

Pete Vedic smiled. Brunkman was pulling away. He'd talked his way out of it. Vedic's smile got broader. Les was heading up the south slope of the canyon, riding straight toward him. He'd be the one who'd have the fun of stopping Les, calling his hand.

Dropping his leg, he wheeled his horse in behind a clump of thorny bush briar to wait.

Halfway out of the canyon, Les Brunkman looked back. Ev Feak had resumed his seat in the buggy. His brother was staring up the slope as though having a final yearning look at the money he had provided. The two punchers stood off to one side. He'd have no trouble with any of them. He stirred contentedly.

Five thousand dollars!

Not exactly a big fortune, he thought, but it would keep him and Melly eating high on the hog in Mexico for a long time. Maybe he'd try to run it into more. He'd always had good luck with the faro tables in Juárez City.

He frowned, thinking of the girl. He had a bit of a problem facing him there that needed straightening out. She'd changed since Ledbetter had moved in, tried to take her over. But he'd fix that. He'd damn quick let her know she belonged to him — and show her how he took care of anybody who tried to buck him.

He hoped Ledbetter had come back looking for her, and had walked into the trap he'd set up. Working that big four-flusher over would be a good way to show her that he didn't fool around none.

And once she'd seen him in action she'd settle down, behave. Be good having her around, real good to spend time with. Not the best-looking woman he'd ever tied up with, but she was young and built well and hadn't been through the mill like the others.

He grinned, thinking of Pete Vedic. Old Pete would be sitting back at the hotel waiting for him to show up with the money; or it could be he'd got a mite nervous about the deal and gone to Bear Paw Crossing; regardless, he was holding the sack on a snipe hunt. Pete was out of luck. And to make it even better, Les wasn't only walking off with the money but with the girl, too.

Pete had wanted Melly bad, and Brunkman guessed he couldn't blame him for kicking Florinda out, but Pete would have to dig himself up somebody else. Melly wasn't for him. . . . Maybe this little jolt would make old Pete realize he wasn't anywhere near the big man he thought he was, that things had changed in the last ten, twelve years. Pete should've known he couldn't be the top dog forever.

Brunkman looked ahead. The rim of the canyon was in sight. He dug spurs into his horse, urged him on. He was anxious to get back to the cabin, anxious to see if Ledbetter was there. Most likely he would be; for all his reputation as a killer, the man had a soft spot. It was going to be a real pleasure squaring things with him, a real pleasure. Time he got through, that big four-flusher folks called the Widowmaker would have to use both hands to hold a gun, much less make a fast draw.

He felt his horse bunch his hindquarters, lunge over the lip of the slope, and come onto level ground. Resettling himself, Brunkman again applied the spurs — and then hauled the horse to a sliding stop.

Something had moved in the brush to his right. Jerking out his pistol, he veered off, and as he did so a bullet whistled past him. He had a quick glimpse of Pete Vedic, the man's round, red-lidded eyes burning at him. Brunkman fired twice in rapid succession.

Vedic's arms flew up as both bullets smashed into his chest, and the pistol he held pitched off into the brush. Brunkman wheeled by for a closer look. Pete glared up at him, his lips working convulsively as they fought to shape words with which to vent hatred.

"You — you back-stabbing bastard," he managed, brushing weakly at the blood-flecked froth bubbling from his mouth. "Florinda — had you — pegged. . . . But — won't get you — nothing. . . ."

"Not much. Only the five thousand and the girl. And anything else of yours I want," Brunkman said dryly.

Pete Vedic's eyes wavered. The skin covering his face grew taut, his teeth bared in a mirthless grin. "Not everything . . . Florinda . . . You'll never get her. . . . She'll kill — you first."

Brunkman laughed. "Never get the chance —" he began, then checked his words. The outlaw leader was dead. Les stared down at him for a moment or two, savoring his triumph. Then, realizing that others of the gang would be close by somewhere, he leaned forward and began to flog his horse into a hard run.

When he reached the edge of the clearing he drew up short. He listened briefly for sounds of pursuit, heard none, and decided Vedic had been alone after all. He turned then to the clearing. Yancey was sitting on the ground near the hitchrack, rubbing at his head in a dazed way. . . . Anger shot through Brunkman. God-damn that Yancey — he'd let Ledbetter trick him!

He rode forward and pulled up beside the man, dropped to the ground. Shaking him roughly, he said: "What the hell's going on?"

Yancey stared at him stupidly. "Ledbetter," he mumbled. "Hit me with something. . . . Got my iron."

Furious, Les glanced to the cabin. "The girl, what about her?"

"Took her. . . ."

"Where?" Brunkman demanded, slapping Yancey savagely across the face. "Where?"

"Don't — know. . . . Didn't see nothing. . . ."

Brunkman rose, turned to his horse. Ledbetter would head for Chacosa. It was his only choice, and he wouldn't have much of a start. They'd follow the road because of the girl, and if he cut across the hills, got in ahead of them. . . .

"Les — give me a hand," Yancey mumbled. "Bastard hit me — up side of the head — with my gun. Must've done something bad. . . . Real dizzy. . . ."

Brunkman gave him a short glance and went to the saddle. "Other things I've got to do," he said, and spurred across the clearing.

23

On the crest of a hill a short quarter mile from Chacosa, Ledbetter and Melanie Feak paused to rest their horses.

"I hoped I'd never see that place again," she murmured, staring down at the sun-drenched buildings.

"Had a few doubts about it myself," Aaron replied with a wry grin.

She considered him soberly. "Was all that true, what you said about the marshal forcing you to go after me?"

He nodded. "That bit of trouble I had in town — he used it like a club over my head."

"And now that it's all straightened out you'll move on . . . to El Paso."

"That was the deal."

Melanie turned her head, looked off over the gently rolling hills seemingly stretching to infinity beyond the settlement.

"Can't — couldn't you stay? I thought that maybe we . . ."

Her words trailed into nothing. He pushed back his hat, studied her closely. The lines of his face deepened as understanding came to him.

"You're a nice girl," he said slowly, "and not cut out for my kind of life. Same as you weren't meant to throw in with Vedic and his crowd. You learned that."

"A woman becomes a part of her husband's life, no matter what it is, if she loves him."

Ledbetter's shaggy brows lifted. His lips pulled into a cynical, harsh line, and his eyes hardened. A moment later the expression vanished.

"The right man will come along, Melanie. . . . A good man — one who'll deserve you. Don't jump at everyone you meet. That's not love — that's desperation."

She stirred, brushed wearily at a stray wisp of hair blowing against her cheek. "Perhaps. But there are times when I'd settle for anything."

Ledbetter nodded. "Expect everybody goes through that when they're young. . . . Ready?"

Melanie murmured her assent, and together they rode off the summit and down the road leading to the settlement. Aaron glanced back. There had been no pursuit. He guessed Les Brunkman had not returned to the cabin as soon as he'd anticipated; he and Melanie had escaped with time to spare.

He was glad of that. He had no real quarrel with the outlaw — at least none serious enough to warrant killing the man. The hostility was all on Brunkman's part. He looked ahead. They were entering a strip of trees and brush lying in the swale between two storm-cut bluffs. Chacosa was just beyond — and not far apparently, as he could hear faint sounds of activity.

He'd take Melanie to Sam Back's office immediately, using the alleyway to avoid subjecting
the girl to embarrassment as much as possible.
The lawman would see that she got home safely.
As for himself, he couldn't shake the dust of
Chacosa from his boots quick enough; he'd seen
all of that town he ever wanted to.

The growth began to thin as they drew nearer
the opposite side. He slid a glance to Melanie.
Her features were pale, set. He hadn't given it
any thought, but he reckoned she was about all
in from the sleepless night and hard riding.
Likely she'd welcome home now.

Vague motion at the side of the road sent a
quick warning racing through Ledbetter. A rider
bolted suddenly into view on his right. Startled,
the black shied to the left, came up against
Melanie's dapple.

Brunkman!

Aaron's hand swept down for his pistol. In
that identical instant Melanie uttered a low cry,
threw herself at him.

"Look out!" he snarled, and shook her off savagely.

But the split second of opportunity was lost.
Wordless, Ledbetter watched her draw back,
face stilled, eyes downcast.

"Obliged to you, honey, helping me like that,"
Les Brunkman said, grinning broadly, "but
wasn't no need. Had him covered all the time."

Aaron continued to stare at the girl. That she
had deliberately interfered, prevented his using

his weapon, was unquestionable. After a moment he shook his head. He thought she had learned, had changed her thinking. He had been wrong.

"Get his gun — then come on over here," the outlaw continued. "We're all set for Mexico. I got the money — even took care of old Pete. . . . And soon as I take care of this jasper, we'll line out."

Melanie raised her head to Ledbetter. Eyes filled with misery, she said, "I'm sorry. I couldn't do it. I couldn't go back."

He gave her no reply, sat motionless while she took his weapon and crossed to Brunkman.

"Maybe I ought to let you keep this," Les said, taking the pistol from her. "Feather in my cap was folks to learn how I'd cut down the fancy-shooting Widowmaker."

Ledbetter shrugged. "Better hang onto it. You'll need it to shoot me in the back," he said, and waited for the effect of his words.

Brunkman's eyes narrowed, and he laughed harshly. "Still the big talker, eh?"

"Met your kind before," Aaron said coolly. "Long as you've got the edge, you're running over with strong words."

Melanie, suddenly aware, said: "Do you have to kill him? Can't we just ride on — let him go? He hasn't done anything — really."

"Nothing but push me around — and I don't take that from nobody!"

"But there's no reason —"

"Keep out of this, goddamn it!" Brunkman snapped, anger tearing at his broad face.

Melanie looked down at her hands. The outlaw glared at her briefly, then swung his attention reflectively to Aaron. A half grin cracked his lips.

"Tell you what, mister, I'll give you a chance to prove you're fast as folks claim."

Ledbetter listened in silence. Any break Les Brunkman offered him likely would be less than none at all.

"I'm going to toss you your gun, your own gun," Les said, drawing Aaron's pistol from his belt. "We'll see if you can catch it and shoot before I can pull the trigger of mine."

"Right generous of you," Ledbetter said dryly.

"Better'n nothing at all."

Again Aaron stirred indifferently. "You want to make it look good, holster your gun. Still have all the odds."

The outlaw grunted. "Look good to who?"

Ledbetter, fighting for even the smallest chance, pointed at Melanie. "To her — and to yourself. Shoot me down cold and you'll never know whether you're fast as me or not."

Les Brunkman stiffened angrily. "Ain't no doubt in my mind about that — but you got yourself a deal."

Aaron felt the faintest glimmering of hope. It wouldn't help much, he knew, but it could afford him an extra second or two, unless, of course, the outlaw nullified it all by deliberately making a bad throw. Tensing in the saddle, he nodded.

"Anytime you're ready."

Instantly Melanie turned to Brunkman, pulled at his arm. "No, Les — don't! He was only trying to help!"

Keeping his weapon leveled at Aaron, the outlaw knocked her hands aside. "Get out of the way!" he snapped.

"No — I won't let you —"

The outlaw slapped her hard across the face, sent her reeling in the saddle. He grinned viciously at Ledbetter, giving no more thought to the girl, now sobbing quietly.

"Say your prayers, mister," he muttered, holstering his gun, and then, with a quick flip of his other hand, sent Ledbetter's weapon spinning through the air.

Aaron threw himself from the saddle. In the briefest fragment of time he had gauged the weapon's path. The blast of Brunkman's pistol and the searing flight of its bullet across his arm reached him at the same time his outstretched fingers wrapped around the butt of his descending gun. He ducked under the shying, frightened black. From one knee he fired once — fired again. Les Brunkman stared down at him, a surprised look on his face. For a long, breathless moment the outlaw held himself rigid, and then, wilting, he fell heavily to the ground.

Ledbetter got to his feet slowly, tension still holding him in its tight grasp. He glanced toward

Melanie, felt a wave of surprise wash through him. Just beyond the girl Marshal Sam Back, rifle in hand, stood in the road.

And from the street beyond the edge of the brush a voice shouted: "Hey! What was that shooting?"

24

The lawman moved in slowly, rifle pointing at Aaron Ledbetter.

"Everything's fine," he said in a quiet voice. "Just fine. Reckon you'd better drop that gun."

Ledbetter's jaw hardened. He stared at the marshal for several momenta and then, shrugging, allowed his weapon to fall.

"Seen you coming over the hill," Sam Back continued. "Was waiting — but I didn't know this bird was hiding in the brush." He nudged Brunkman with his toe. "Who is he?"

"One of Vedic's bunch."

The old lawman nodded. "Sure was rearing for you. I hear him say he'd killed Vedic?"

"What he said."

There was the quick sound of oncoming horses. Sam Back glanced toward the town, swung his attention once more to Aaron and Melanie.

"Both of you — just stand easy now."

Two riders appeared suddenly at the bend in the road, pulled to a halt. Both swept the scene with startled eyes.

"By thunder, the marshal's gone and done it!" one shouted, abruptly recovering. "He's got the killer and Ev's girl — just like he said he'd do!"

"And he got hisself another of them out-laws, too!" the second man chimed in. "You needing help, Marshal?" he added, spurring up closer.

Behind him his partner wheeled about and started for town, shouting at the top of his voice.

Sam Back greeted the newcomer with a curt bob of his head. "Get over there, Ernie, pick up that gun and fetch it to me."

Ernie, face serious, obediently trotted to where Ledbetter stood, scooped up the weapon, returned it to the lawman. Back took it by the barrel, never for an instant lowering his rifle. More shouting was now coming from the street, and mixed with it, the sound of running.

Aaron, weariness beginning to weigh on him, conscious of the dull pain in his arm where Brunkman's bullet had sliced its groove, shifted impatiently. "Reckon this clears me —"

"Never you mind!" the lawman broke in loudly. "I'll do the talking." He ducked his head at Melanie. "Come over here, girl."

Melanie crossed silently to where Back and the man called Ernie stood. A dozen or so persons abruptly hove into view behind them, hesitated briefly, and then rushed forward. All began to speak at once, hurling questions, tendering congratulations.

Sam Back took it in grand style. Finally he raised his hand and turned to the girl.

"They do you any harm?"

Melanie, white and drawn, said, "I'm all

right." She glanced to Aaron. "But you're wrong about —"

"Kaseman!" the lawman shouted, ignoring her hurriedly, and probing the crowd. "Putting this girl in your charge. See she gets home." He added quickly: "And don't go bothering her with no questions. She's all worn-out."

An elderly man pushed through the group. He smiled up at Melanie, took the dapple's bridle in his hand. "Be pleased to, Marshal," he said. "Sure glad she's all right. Be a powerful relief to Ev and his missus."

Back nodded as if that, too, had been due to his efforts. "You can tell Ev I got the money. He can pick it up at my office."

Ledbetter watched the old lawman while a mixture of irritation and amusement moved through him. It had finally dawned on his jaded mind; Sam Back was making it appear to one and all that he had effected a capture and rescued Melanie Feak — and he was doing a good job of it, making the most of every moment. Aaron wondered what Sam would do if Melanie wanted to tell a different version of her rescue, then realized he'd have the means of keeping her quiet. The marshal had witnessed the scene with Brunkman, knew that the girl had been aiming to go off with the outlaw. She wouldn't exactly want folks to know about that.

A faint grin tugged at the corners of his mouth as another thought came to him. How would the marshal explain him? Sam had promised him freedom, but to the townspeople he was an escaped prisoner and a horse thief.

He came to sharp attention. Three riders rode slowly from the brush, halted at the edge of the road. He touched them with his glance. Vedic's men. One was Kansas, the others he did not know by name. Evidently they had been trailing Brunkman and blundered onto the scene in the grove. He watched them take in Brunkman's lifeless body with a quick look, settle their hard gaze on the lawman.

Sam Back, all business, shifted his eyes to Ledbetter. "Who're they?" he demanded crisply.

Aaron considered the situation — the old lawman and his rifle, three heavily armed outlaws. He shook his head.

"Ask them."

Back wheeled to the three men. After a moment Kansas shrugged. "Just passing through, Marshal," he said in an offhand way.

"You got business in my town?"

The outlaw stirred indifferently. "Not specially. . . . Like I said, was just riding by —"

"Then keep riding!" the lawman snapped. "Got myself enough problems around here without you drifters cluttering up the place."

Kansas smiled. He turned slightly toward Ledbetter, winked, and then, swinging about, led the others back into the brush.

Immediately the crowd broke into excited conversation. Someone slapped the old lawman heartily on the back.

"By heaven, Sam — you're all right!"

"You see how he run off them hardcases? Cool as you please. Bet if that Vedic showed up —"

"Vedic's dead — same as that one laying there on the ground," the marshal said flatly.

There was a moment of stunned silence, and then more cheering erupted. A man shoved his way to the front of the gathering.

"You mean you broke up that outlaw gang for sure?"

"Expect so. With Pete Vedic gone ain't much to hold them together."

The yelling continued. Someone said: "Wait'll Harvey Kitchell hears about that. Sure going to do a lot of eating crow!"

More praise poured onto the lawman. Ernie, apparently assuming deputy duties, pointed to Ledbetter.

"What about him, Marshal? Want me to take him in, lock him up?"

Sam Back lowered his rifle for the first time. "Got to studying on that," he said, frowning. "Ain't really got much against him . . . and it could get the town in a passel of trouble, false arrest, and such."

Ernie stared incredulously. "You aiming to let him go?"

"Ain't much else I can do. Some of you folks right here seen what happened in the Castlerock. Was pure self-defense — and he couldn't help it none if Amos got in the way of a stray bullet."

"But the kidnapping —"

"Wasn't none of his doing. That was Vedic."

"Yes, but you trailed him right up to Vedic's hangout —"

"Sure, we trailed him that direction. Ain't but one road out there, you know that. Same as you know he didn't ride in here till yesterday — and from the north. Plain he ain't one of the gang."

Aaron Ledbetter sighed quietly. He'd heard enough, had enough. Sam Back had made his point, the girl was again with her parents — and he was free to go. Maybe he'd been the goat, but he guessed his pride could stand that.

He walked up to the lawman, extended his hand. "I'll take my gun."

Sam Back met his gaze squarely, faint question in his eyes. Passing over the weapon, he said, "Your horse is standing there in the brush. Was using him myself seeing as how you took mine."

Ledbetter holstered his pistol, moved toward the edge of the road. Sam Back's voice, stern and uncompromising, reached him.

"Now — want you to keep going. Letting you off on the strength of that."

Temper began to stir within Aaron Ledbetter. Someone in the crowd laughed, slapped his palms together.

"Sam's sure got the fire when he needs it — I'll say that much!"

"And don't be coming back this way," the lawman continued in the same harsh tone. "My town's closed to you. Understand?"

"Jesus! He's talking that way to the *Widowmaker!*"

Ledbetter wheeled slowly, all patience drained from him. Instantly the crowd fell into a hush. Sam Back stiffened perceptibly. Color appeared in his neck, began to spread into his slack cheeks; and his eyes, suddenly visibly old, filled with an earnestness that craved understanding, begged for sympathy and a pardon, if in his zeal to revive his fading prestige he had overplayed his hand.

Aaron Ledbetter studied the aging lawman for several deadly quiet moments, and then shrugged.

"Sure, Marshal," he said, and moved on.

The employees of G.K. Hall hope you have enjoyed this Large Print book. All our Large Print titles are designed for easy reading, and all our books are made to last. Other G.K. Hall books are available at your library, through selected bookstores, or directly from us.

For information about titles, please call:

(800) 223-1244
(800) 223-6121

To share your comments, please write:

Publisher
G.K. Hall & Co.
P.O. Box 159
Thorndike, ME 04986